What You've Been Missing

The

John

Simmons

Short

Fiction

Award

University of

Iowa Press

Iowa City

*Janet
Desaulniers*

*What
You've Been
Missing*

University of Iowa Press, Iowa City 52242
Printed in the United States of America
http://www.uiowa.edu/uiowapress
The publication of this book was generously supported by the
National Endowment for the Arts.

The University of Iowa Press is a member of Green Press
Initiative and is committed to preserving natural resources.
Printed on acid-free paper

Library of Congress Cataloging-in-Publication Data
Desaulniers, Janet, 1954–.
    What you've been missing / by Janet Desaulniers.
       p.   cm.—(The John Simmons short fiction award)
    Contents: Where we all should have been—The good
fight—Everyone is wearing a hat—Real love—The next
day—Mothers without children—Roll—Never, ever,
always—After Rosa Parks—Who knows more than you.
    ISBN 0-87745-910-X
    1. United States—Social life and customs—Fiction.
I. Title. II. Series
PS3604.E757W48 2004
813'.6—dc22   2004046068

04   05   06   07   08   P   5   4   3   2

Luke and Michael

proof and permission

Contents

ACKNOWLEDGMENTS

The following stories first appeared, some in different form, in these publications: "Everyone Is Wearing a Hat," "The Good Fight," and "Where We All Should Have Been" in the *New Yorker*; "Never, Ever, Always" and "After Rosa Parks" in *Ploughshares*; "Roll" in the *New England Review*; "The Next Day" in *TriQuarterly*; and "Mothers without Children" in *Glimmer Train*.

Many thanks to the editors of those publications and to the Henfield Foundation, the Michener/Copernicus Society, the Illinois Arts Council, and the National Endowment for the Arts for their generous support.

Thanks and love to Annette Desaulniers-Barczewski, Sara Levine, Don Michie, Arthur Morey, and Sally Savic, who understood it was their job to remain calm.

What You've Been Missing

Where
We All
Should
Have Been

The last time my mother called she did not say hello. She said, "This is not a discussion, Ellen. I need you here. It's Diana. She drinks. And God knows what else. This morning she came in near dawn, wobbling in this awful way and smelling musty, damp—I can't describe it—and looking like something you find at the bottom of the clothes hamper. She didn't say a word, just wandered from lamp to lamp snapping them off. When she came to the pole lamp near the chair I'd been sitting in I felt so odd, almost terrified. I said to her, 'Diana, I'm here,' and she looked at me and said, 'Oh, sorry. I didn't see you,' just as blasé as a cat. I'm telling you, Ellen, I've thought of everything. I've thought of drugs, but drugs don't leave a musty odor. Or do they?"

"None that I know of," I said.

"See, that's why you must come home. You understand children this age. You're the ranking expert. I haven't the mind for this."

She was referring to my job—which was juvenile social worker—and she was wrong. I was no expert. I saw twelve-year-olds who had blazed trails of mistake so twisted and confounding that I was stupefied. "Send up a flare," I once told a boy who lazed in my office chair. "You're going to have to show me where you are on this planet." Weeks later he killed his dog, then roamed the length of his alleyway aiming a target pistol at women and children.

"It could be anything," I told my mother. "Maybe just a wrong-headed risk, maybe nothing at all."

"Just please do not tell me it's a reaction to your father's death, all right? Everybody is an analyst all of a sudden—from those damn nuns to her bus driver. 'She's reacting to her father's death,' they say. 'Tell me about it,' I say. But it's precious little help when it comes to finding out where she's been until all hours. The child is *missing*. She sits right in front of me and is not there."

"Listen," I said. "Mom."

She stopped. Actually, she seized the silence. Then she said, "Don't. Do not, all right? I'm fifty-seven years old. I know the way the world feels before the other shoe drops. Trust me on this."

"Look," she went on. "I won't say I can't lose any more. That would be stupid. You've lost enough to understand how stupid that would be."

She wasn't talking then only about the loss of my father. She was talking also about my brief marriage, which my husband had left vaguely, turning off the sausages I was cooking one morning and sitting me down. "It doesn't feel right," he told me. None of the rest of what he said made any more sense than that. My mother believed I understood now, as certainly as she did, that life was one loss slowly opening into another.

"So I won't say I can't lose any more," my mother said. "But I will say this. I will say I can't lose any more alone."

"OK," I told her. "I'll be there Friday. I'll take a sick day and leave early."

"Good," she said. "Thank you. All right. Hooray. I'm going to put Diana on now and then I'm going to bed."

"Diana?" I said. "You mean she's there?"

"Yes."

"Right there? She's listening?"

"Ellen, if I could, I would take the child's bedroom door off its hinges. It's the secrets I want to get rid of."

Once my mother had liked secrets. Once she herself had seemed to me to be a secret. Whenever I'd pressed with questions about boys she'd known or men she'd loved her mouth closed in a lovely line, urging restraint and silence. On special occasions even her gowns and small silk shoes, dyed some shy pastel shade, seemed secrets that might one day, with luck, be mine.

Now age had made her raise her voice, or maybe it was only the telephone. We were a long-distance family—three women trying to locate one another in that strange space of absence between two cocked receivers. I squinted during all her calls. I'm sure she did, too. My sister Diana, who was sixteen, squinted even across a room.

"I'm putting her on now," she said.

I heard them exchange the receiver, but Diana didn't say anything.

"Diana," I said. "What's going on? Is it Dad, Diana?"

She wasn't going to tell me.

"Diana, say something."

"I don't know what to say," she told me. "You had better say something."

"It's going to be OK."

"No, it's not." She sat silent again for a long minute, then hung up. A few moments later she called back.

"It's not Dad," she told me. "I want that clear. It is not Dad, but if he were it, I'd say this to you. I'd say that after he died I could read your mind. You were walking around thinking, This is the worst time of my life. I'm divorced and now my father is *dead.*" She said the word vengefully, as if I'd forced her to say it. "You were thinking, This has to be it. The bottom. The worst. It's over. Then you went marching off to make a new start. Well, I think that stinks. I think you stink. I'm still here, you know." She lowered her voice, and I understood that my mother had not yet gone to bed. "I'm still here with her."

"Diana."

"I'm going to hang up on you again."

"OK," I told her.

"All right," she said and did it.

That Friday, Kansas City was a gentle town to drive into—full of transitions, nothing bold; the flat farmland eased into a roll of hills, the Missouri swung through, and there it was: a skyline you could hold in one eye.

I paid my toll on the Broadway Bridge to a woman whose nameplate read "Ellowese." She smiled at me, tapped two nickels out of a handful into my palm, and as I crossed the river, the bridge surface clicking under my tires, I sat up and smiled back. There, to my right, in front of the old American Hereford building, serious, stolid, balanced on a pylon, was my father's favorite statue, the biggest statue of a bull I'd ever seen. Whenever we passed it on long car rides, my father had liked to tell the story of its construction: how when it went up it faced east, but then there had been problems with Kansas and the view of its hind end they had over there. Someone even made a speech about it in the state senate. So it was rolled around to face north and had stood up there since, a red light between its ears to ward off airplanes. It cheered me up to see it, made me feel safe, home, acquainted with the front and back doors. Ahead was a bull with its backside pointed in a diplomatic direction. Behind was a woman who spelled her name "Ellowese."

My mother had sold the old house and bought an apartment I'd not yet seen, in a midtown complex of hotels, shops, and condominiums. The entryway to her building was carpeted, canopied, decked with small trees, and watched over by a slight stooped man in a gold coat. He charmed me through the lobby, carried my bag to the elevator, and then reached inside it to punch the floor for me.

"Welcome home, now," he said, and handed me a key.

After the doors closed, I thought of our old house—a city house with a warped front porch, a scrubby patch of lawn, two elm trees, and a sparsely graveled driveway leading back to a garage near the alley. Changes in circumstances always frightened me a little. Just before I left town after my marriage my father had lingered with me at the front door.

"You be good," he told me, his hand light on my shoulder, "and stick to the path." He shook me gently. "You remember Harry Truman was a little haberdasher who left home and dropped the bomb."

———

The apartment had double doors, burnished oak with two brass knockers. I went in feeling ill-advised, half expecting someone like Loretta Young to come sweeping out to meet me. When I saw the grandfather clock from the old house I closed the door behind me. The place had a view. Just past the living and dining rooms, past overstuffed furniture and glass end tables I'd never seen, the city rose up in sharp right angles through a wide picture window. It looked substantial, right outside the window like that. While I was standing there, the clock, which had never worked in my lifetime, struck four. No one was home.

I went into my mother's room. Except for pictures of my sister and me, it was completely new, low-slung and contemporary in black and white. Everything looked exact, definite, consciously placed: crystal perfume bottles spaced so evenly they seemed to quiver, one shrill note shy of shattering. I could hear my own breath, and then I heard someone at the door.

It was Diana. She cursed quietly as I came down the hall and saw her, bent over, back to me, trying to work the key out of the door.

"Hey," I said. "Hi."

She jerked upright, slammed the door with her key still in it, and stood there breathing softly into her hand as though she needed to assure herself.

"Jesus." She touched her throat and forehead lightly. "I forgot about you."

She threw her books under the hat rack and slumped into a

chair at the end of the dining table, pressing her forearms against her temples.

"Wait," she said. "Give me a minute."

I stood still and saw that she was taller, thinner, had let her hair grow, and that her hands trembled faintly just around the wrists. When she lifted her head to look at me, though, her hair fell away from her face to a sharp smile.

"What?"

"Nothing. The ghosts don't usually show up this early, is all."

"Ghosts," I said. "This place is one minute old. I'm not sure some of the doorknobs have fingerprints on them."

"Ha." She leaned back in her chair. "It is spooky." She stretched her legs in front of her, put her hands in her pockets, then looked at me. "Hey, do you have a cigarette? The bus driver took my cigarettes."

I found my pack, brought it and an ashtray to her chair, then offered my lighter. She did not look like someone from whom a bus driver could take anything. Extreme is how she looked. She was dressed all in black—light jacket, loose sweater, jeans, and short leather boots. Even her hair looked darker, folding down to her shoulders and cut in spikes around her face. Against it her skin was so pale she looked ill and defiant. She smoked the cigarette, between thumb and forefinger, like a pretty gangster.

I sat down next to her at the table.

"Didn't the doorman tell you I was up here?"

"I came in the back way," she said. "Old Solomon bugs me. I had a drink with him a couple nights, and now he thinks we're buddies."

"You drink with our mother's doorman."

"Twice." She gave me a smile I recognized and then let it fade to caution. "Just two times. Not at a bar or anything. I just sat with him down there. He's got a wastebasket full of ice and a bottle under a copy of the paper. Anyway, he's not a bad guy, really. He says he knew Bennie Moten. He knows all these facts, too—like did you know a yardbird was a chicken?"

"I knew that," I said, "and you know our mother did not mortgage the farm so that you could drink with her doorman."

She made a tinny sound in the back of her throat like a laugh swallowed. "You're right there." Slipping her boots off she nudged them across the parquet floor to the hat rack and stared at them. I watched them with her.

Then she looked over at me earnestly. "Listen," she said. "Do you care if I play some music?"

"No."

"She kept the old stereo." Diana said, already out of her chair. "It remedies my day. All those nuns, you know."

"Sure."

She played a Count Basie record, an old one, so scratchy the music seemed trapped inside a wall of rain. Diana seemed to be inside the rain with it. She sat in a wing chair she'd turned to face the picture window, and, both bare feet propped on the sill, she stared out over her toes at the afternoon traffic. Sunlight fell on her, dazzling her hair and blurring her profile. I wondered if she was trying to welcome me home in some distant way. I hadn't heard a Count Basie record in our house since Diana and I were little. Then my mother had liked to tidy up to his music. She'd played it loud, too, in those days, the house swelling with sound and my mother moving absently through rooms. She'd empty a few ashtrays, scrub a pot, run a cloth over tabletops, but distantly, far away, as if she'd been transported; I was never sure where, though as a child I imagined some late-night place where ladies sat at tables in a pink glow, didn't wear gloves, and glanced over their shoulders just so—someplace where it was always after hours, that same beat, the same smoky room, someone frying pork chops in the back.

Before the record finished on the first side the phone in the kitchen rang twice then stopped. Diana turned the music off, and the silence was sudden, as though the building had just dropped out of a storm.

"That's Solomon's signal," she said. "She's home."

"I'm home," my mother said a moment later from the door. "Who left a key in the door?"

I stood up at the table as she came in. Holding a bag of take-out barbecue, she kissed me on the mouth and looked at me in a genuine way, brightly, eye to eye.

"Hi," she said. "Smile at me."

I smiled.

"There." She touched my cheek gently. "You look fine. Snapshot quality. Thank God. Now we can eat ribs." She passed out the thick paper plates gaily, saying, "I said, 'Make them special, extra sauce. This is a reunion. All my chickens.'"

My mother was a tall, dark-haired woman of high color. Gaiety always made her beautiful and me too shy to mention it. Diana came in from the living room. My mother gave her a quick hard look and placed the key on the table.

"Yours," she said. "And Mrs. Emory was waiting for me at the elevator again. I have given her permission to axe the door and set fire to that stereo the next time you play it so loud, which brings me to whether or not you took the bus home today?"

Diana slid into a chair without even pulling it from the table. She was very thin.

"Yes, ma'am," she said, folding her long hands in front of her. "I sat behind the driver and led a round of 'Row Your Boat.'"

My mother stared. Then her head fell back one notch as if she'd been tapped lightly at the base of the skull.

"I've got beer somewhere," she said, handing me a napkin without breaking her gaze, "though I imagine Diana would prefer a pint of something vile, hold the glass."

"Listen." Diana patted the table twice, waited, then pushed back her chair. "I think I'll eat in the living room."

"Oh, fine. Great. Extraordinarily good." My mother held the napkin over my head. I looked up and saw a flush spread under her chin. "You can drink with us, you know. I'm not going to shoot you for it."

Diana stood at her place, shook her head at the ribs. "I'm going to sit at the window and watch the sunset," she said. "You're supposed to watch the sunset. People write about it in songs." She picked up her plate and looked my mother dead in the face on her way out. "I'll be able to hear every word you say."

"Go," my mother said softly, sitting down next to me. "Watch the damn sunset."

When she was gone my mother sat quietly, crushing the napkin to a ball in her hand and stroking her forearm as if it ached.

"She's different," I said.

My mother didn't look at me. "Aren't we all?" she said.

I sat up straighter, and my mother's hand moved briefly from her forearm to mine.

"Sorry," she said. "Eat. This *is* a reunion. And I'm glad. And I really do think you look fine."

She held up one finger, moved back to the kitchen, and came back with a gallon of milk and two glasses.

"We'll set an example," she said, raising the jug in the direction of the living room. She poured herself half a glass of milk, then stopped.

"She drinks too much for a girl, you know, and straight out of the bottle. I say, 'Diana, a drink in the afternoon can be quieting, but get a glass, for God's sake.' Now she tries not to let me see. She tries not to let me see anything." Looking past me to the living room, she shook her head. "Nights she's just gone. 'To the library,' she'll say. Right. But what? I can't tail her." She filled both glasses with milk and sat down.

"Nevertheless, something's going on. Some nights it's eerie. She comes back talking different. 'Y'all,' she'll say. Once it was 'I reckon.' Who talks like that? *I reckon.* Good God, she's found some blind bartender in a roadside lounge. I don't know." She pressed her hands against the table as if she might get up again.

"She's young," I said.

"Right." She released the pressure on her hands and leaned back in her chair. "Exactly. And I'm old. We are not a matched set."

My mother did not look old to me. She looked like her new furnishings—impeccable, ageless, and fine in a way that made me hesitant and proper—but she did not look old. I saw that she was watching me, waiting for me to tell her so, and I did.

"You look better than ever."

She brightened when I said it, straightened her spine, and smiled. "Oh, it's just the new clothes, the new place. Everything just out of the band-box. But thanks." She waved her hand shyly. "So what do you think? Great, isn't it? Safe, secure, all the conveniences. The whole complex is downright twenty-third century—like a city unto itself. Tonight, for example. Oh." She stopped. "I figured you'd want to rest tonight, so I didn't cancel the evening."

"Fine," I said.

"Well, tonight . . ." She handed me a small tub of coleslaw and a plastic fork. "Tonight I'll have a drink, then dancing at the new hotel, maybe a late snack—all without leaving the building. I won't even muss my hair. It's just the girls from the office for the drink. Actually, I'm late now. We do it every Friday. Gripes, gab, the girls. You know."

She glanced over her shoulder, as if for the first time she didn't want my sister to overhear.

"It's Timmy," she said, turning back to me, "for the dancing."

Standing suddenly with her plate, she asked me in a casual voice if she'd told me about him and if her blouse was too revealing without her jacket. It was a red silk blouse, scooped low in the back and scalloped over the bodice, hanging sleek and perfect, like a blouse you see on an actress in a movie but never think of owning. It did not reveal too much.

Timmy, I thought. A grown man. But I said, "Very pretty. Nice. Fine."

When I said it she stopped and looked at me severely. Then she laid her plate of ribs back on the table, looked at her watch, and sat down, smoothing her skirt. Slowly, she reached for one of my cigarettes, then stopped and stared at me as if she were about to say something. As I waited for her to say it I knew she wasn't going to. I knew Timmy had a room on one of the cheaper floors of the hotel or was exactly like his name, and that it was none of my business.

She sat, staring, long enough for me to take that all in, twice. Then she stood up, gathered her keys, and draped her jacket over one arm.

"Well," she said. "I'm already late."

"Have a good night," I said.

"You too." She opened the front door. "Diana, I'm going, and you're in by midnight, right?"

Diana raised one foot from her chair by the window.

"Right," my mother said, looking at me. "Maybe you two girls can have a nice talk." She said it with grit in her voice, like a dare. Then she closed the door.

I listened after her until I heard the distant ring of the elevator, then looked down at her plate. She hadn't eaten much. Everyone was getting thin, losing weight. When I looked up, I saw Diana, leaning around the chair back, watching me. She gave a half-friendly, half-knowing wave.

"Ready for our nice chat?" she said.

"No." I walked over and sat on the windowsill facing her. She grinned at me, looked expectant.

"Go ahead and smile," I said. "But Lord, Diana—*Timmy*."

"Yeah." She slouched into the chair and crossed her ankles next to me on the sill. "He's that bad, too," she said. Then she sat up again. "Listen—first, I am not a teenage alcoholic, but, second, if you are going to sit there and talk about Timmy, then I deserve a drink." She pulled a pint of something pink out from under the seat cushion. "So do you mind?"

I glanced at the door. "I don't know. No."

"Thanks." She leaned back into the chair, rested the bottle on her chest while she unscrewed the cap, then tipped it to her lips. Her forehead pulled when she drank, made her face serious and intent.

"So you've met him?"

"Sort of." She gasped a little after the drink. "One night we sat here awhile waiting for her to change shoes. He told me he just retired from the Air Force and now he's a travel agent. Then he told me he was thinking of growing a mustache—he'd never had one—and just before she came in he said he'd decided this was going to be Timmy's year."

"Timmy's year. Good God. What did you say?"

"I didn't say anything. He wasn't asking me a question. Anyway, that was it. She had her shoes on and they left."

Diana tipped the bottle again, this time smiling as she drank.

"What is that?" I said.

She held it up so I could see the label.

"'Feeney's Cherry Vodka'," I read. "That's a ridiculous thing to drink."

"I'm aware," she said, looking past me out the window. I turned to look with her and saw the last of the sun disappear behind the city, but I could tell her attention was on the street, as though she were trying to pick out a particular car.

"There's your sunset," I said.

Her eyes moved once to the sky, then settled back on the street. In the half-dark of the room her face was soft, a girl's face, glowing as if she'd just scrubbed it.

"You look pretty in this light," I said, hooking my stocking feet under her seat cushion. "Have you realized yet that you grew up to be pretty?"

She cocked her head at me. "So did you." She nodded behind her to the door. "So did she. How much do you reckon it will save me in ten years?"

"It's only an observation," I said. "Not a prophecy. You really do say 'reckon'. Where did you pick that up?"

She raised the bottle again and shrugged, then looked back at the street.

"Hey," I said, wiggling my foot under the cushion. "Hey, who buys that stuff for you?"

Although she did not blink, she changed when I said it. Her mouth fell open a bit, and she looked up from the street to the night sky. Slowly, pressing the top of the bottle under her chin, she closed her mouth and pulled her lips into a straight, thin line.

"A boy?" I said.

She didn't move.

"A man?"

As a child she could never tell a lie without smiling. A dish would crash in the kitchen and she would follow the sound out to us. "I didn't do it," she'd say, almost beaming, her eyes tearing with the effort to pull her face into control. She wasn't smiling now. Her eyes were dry. She put one foot on the floor, then the other foot next to it, looked down as though she were measuring.

"It's worse than Timmy," she said.

She capped the bottle, slipped it back under the cushion of the chair, and stood up.

"I'm going down to the river for a while," she said. "I've got a ride waiting."

"The river." I stood up with her. "The river is rank, isn't it? Has someone fixed the river?"

She stopped at the hat rack to pull on her boots. "What do you mean? It's a river."

"Well, doesn't it still smell like a chemical plant? Isn't that still the worst part of town?"

"That would be my guess."

"Well, who goes there?"

"I do," she said. "I'll see you."

"Diana." I walked behind her to the door and held it.

"What?" she said.

"You know, whoever he is—I mean, whatever it is you're doing, you don't have to do it."

"I already did," she said and pulled the door closed.

After she'd left I sat in her chair by the window and looked down at the street. I wanted to see her, to note the make of the car, to be a witness, but she wasn't there. I slipped her bottle from under the cushion and held it. Then I unscrewed the top and took a drink. The sweet, thick taste made me wince. It was unimaginable. I recapped the bottle. The clock chimed seven behind me, and I stood up. Except for the gleam of light over the vacated dining table, the room stretched with long shadows, and I saw it again as a strange room, frozen and unfamiliar. I stared a moment at the chairs and tables, at the plates of abandoned food, the stillness so profound it stilled me. Then I put Diana's bottle in my pocket and left.

I drove around for hours, making a wide circle past parks we'd played in as children, past the Catholic girls' school that we attended. Lingering at crosswalks I examined the faces illuminated by my headlights. Through downtown I drove slowly, idling in front of bars, watching shadows flicker in and out of lighted doorways. Down at the river I smelled the musty, dank odor that had mystified my mother when she smelled it on Diana. It was the stench of mud, oil, and industry. Nothing much was down there—empty lots, rubbish shifting in the breeze, the blackened shell of a gas station, and, in the distance, the flame and haze of the refinery. I drove back into the city and ended up on Twelfth Street outside the Manhattan Bar, a squat and oddly whimsical dive with a checkerboard façade that sat across from the YMCA. I'd given up on finding Diana. I was just sitting in my parked car, thinking dully of my father and the years he'd come down to the Y every Sunday after Mass for a steam bath and massage.

I was coming to some distant understanding that I'd never have access to the mystery of motive behind his choice to separate the weeks of his adult life that way, with a ritual of prayer, steam, and pummeling, when I heard a woman's laughter, like a tin bell in the dark. Diana was not the one laughing, but the woman who was held the checkerboard door of the Manhattan open and drew Diana inside.

Diana didn't see me come in and take a seat at the bar. She sat, her back to the door, at a table in a far corner. With her was a man, older, my age, filling shot glasses from a bottle of Wild Turkey. He wasn't a dark or deadly looking man. As he leaned into the light suspended over the table, I saw a tiny ribbon of pale scalp around his ears and at his neck; he'd just had a haircut. Diana was smiling and listening raptly to the woman who owned the laugh—a large woman dressed in a garish orange and lime green sweater. As I watched, the woman stood, held up her glass, and made a toast that convulsed all of them. The man with the haircut roared. Diana put her head down on the table.

"What?" the woman said louder. She smiled slowly. "What? Is that too many?" She knocked on Diana's head. "Come on. Fourteen is too many? Tell me."

I watched her and thought stupidly for a moment, Fourteen what? Then the man sneaked both arms around her waist. He pulled her close, leaning back to watch her face as he ran one hand down the inside of her leg.

"One shy of enough," I watched him say.

That's when Diana lifted her head, looked over her shoulder, and saw me.

"Get out of here," she said when she came to stand by my barstool. I was still watching the woman, who had lowered her glass but remained standing, looking into it.

"Jesus, Diana," I said.

"What?"

I turned to her. She looked the same as she had earlier when she stood at our mother's front door—like the tough girl she was trying to be. She made me angry, and I was glad I had embarrassed her in front of those ridiculous people.

"I've been looking for you," I said. I lifted the bottle of cherry vodka from my pocket. "I followed your scent. I even went to the river. You were right. It is still the worst part of town. Or maybe this is." I shook my head at her. "You know, I can't believe I found you."

She put her weight on one hip. "Well, you did."

"I see you're unimpressed. Well, I find it notable. Think about it. I never found the dog when he wandered. I never found the keys when our mother prayed to St. Anthony. I don't even think I believed I'd find you. I was just parked out there."

"That's why you found me then."

"What?"

She leaned forward and spoke through her teeth. "You weren't really *looking* for me."

I shook my head at her. "Diana don't be bright. Don't be clever. Get out of here, OK? That's the YMCA across the street."

"You get out of here." She moved closer to me. "You're the one who thinks she's so bright. In one day you find your way home and you find your little sister."

"OK." I held up my hands. "I get it. But just tell me how this is a solution."

"I'm not telling you anything. Go on." Suddenly she looked behind me, and her voice dropped. "Get out of here, all right?"

I swiveled around on my stool and saw the bartender, a square, heavy man, staring solemnly at us, his arms crossed over his wide chest, a white towel thrown over one shoulder. I held up Diana's bottle and wiggled it at him, saying, "If you carry this fine brand, I need one for Little Sheba here. And a scotch for me."

"*Get out.*" Diana slapped the bar hard, and I turned back to her. We both stared a moment; then I swiveled around to the bartender, who put one finger on the end of his thick nose to let us know he liked that idea.

I felt Diana lean into my back; her knuckles pressed against my spine. She stayed that way until the bartender turned away from us and moved down the bar. Then on my neck I felt her whisper, clenched and insinuating.

"I am not getting thrown out of here for you," she said.

I spun around and grabbed her wrist so hard that she stumbled.

"You're sixteen years old." I said it loud, into her face, squeezing her wrist. "You're barely born, sitting over there with people you shouldn't meet in a lifetime."

"Hush, will you? Just please shut up and leave." She touched my hand on her wrist, and I realized how tightly I held her. "You're hurting me," she said.

I let go of her wrist, and she looked away from me, out over the barroom, faintly shaking her head, her breath and eyes moist.

"Come on, Diana." I touched her elbow lightly. "Please. Let's go, OK?"

She pulled her arm away from me. "Don't touch me again," she said.

"Diana, I am not leaving without you."

"Then stay." She pushed away from the bar, pointing at me. "But right where you are. Don't you come near me."

Men pulled their feet out of the aisle as she walked back to the far corner of the bar. The bartender still stared at me, and I understood that he would not bring me a drink. To spite him I smoked a cigarette and watched Diana's table. No one looked at me, but suddenly the large woman stood and headed for the back, sliding delicately between chairs, her arms held high and away from her hips, as though she moved through a thicket. When she passed me, I stood and followed her.

The ladies' room was a tiny cell, tiled in pink and black and noxious with a baffling fruity scent that knocked me against the back wall. The woman stood in front of me, pressed against the basin, examining her hair in the mirror. She glanced at me, then began to spray her hair with some potion she'd removed from a zippered cosmetic bag imprinted with Dalmatians. Around her face, which was duller and flatter than Diana's, the spray made her black hair glisten in the harsh light of the room. She twisted particular strands, pulling them into odd shapes, which she then appraised intently. When she noticed me watching her, she turned around.

"Do you want to use the sink?"

"Nice hair," I said.

She looked back at her reflection and lifted her chin. "Well, it's this." She held up the spray bottle. "That, and I only comb it every couple days. That's my real secret." She looked at me. "It keeps it wild."

I nodded. She was younger than I thought when I'd watched her in the bar, and that fact exhausted me. She was only a schoolgirl, probably Diana's age, with a young girl's nervous hands and eyes, flickering and wary. As I watched she began to spray more and more of the potion, lifting her hair to find the nape of her neck and the fine smooth spot at each temple. The acrid mist and fruity air brought the awful taste of Diana's pink vodka into my throat. I moved to the basin and eased myself up to sit on the counter facing her.

She stopped, hands in midair. "*What?*"

"No, nothing," I said. "I'm just worn out. Maybe it's this stuff." I slid Diana's bottle from my pocket. "I shouldn't have tasted it." I set the bottle next to me on the counter and looked at her. "Or maybe," I said, "it's those fourteen times you were asking about."

She put the bottle of potion down, her eyes steady now, watching me.

"That's too many," I said. "It really is."

She stiffened. "You're Diana's sister." She shook her hair one time and looked back at her image in the mirror. "I saw you two out there, darling."

With that last word—she pronounced it "dahlin'"—I heard the drawl and breath of a small town. This is who says "reckon," I thought.

"Where are you from?" I asked her. "You're not from around here, are you?"

She smiled and zipped her bottle of spray into her little bag. "My folks run that truck stop you sometimes hear about down in the southwest corner of the state. You know, the one that has the New Year's Eve party every year—free food and coffee and music and all. It's practically in Arkansas. Anyway, they saw me getting restless and sent me up here to my aunt and the nuns. Afraid I'd hop a rig or something."

"You go to the Catholic school?" I said. "With Diana?"

"Sure. What's the matter? Is fourteen too many for a Catholic girl? Or is that just too many for you?"

"OK." I raised my hand. "I'm sorry. I shouldn't have said it."

"No." She picked up her zippered bag, then set it down. "It is too many. I know that." She looked at me and shrugged.

"Listen," I said. "If I could, I'd like to ask you one thing. Is that man out there with you or is he with Diana?"

She gave me a close-lipped smile and shook her head. "I don't think he's decided yet."

"Well, let me just say this. Don't sleep with that man, OK? Don't let Diana sleep with that man."

Her smile weakened, and she ran her hand over her little bag, smoothing it, then setting it upright.

"I'm sorry about what I said. Just don't go off with that man, OK?"

She shrugged again, then lifted herself up on the counter on the other side of the sink. Blankly, she fiddled with the faucet, turning the water on and off so that the pipes shuddered and shook the counter beneath us. Then she stopped and looked up at me. I watched her.

"So you're Diana's sister."

"Yes," I said.

"She doesn't talk about you much."

"Well."

"I never had a sister. My parents are old. They've always been old. My mom says I'm probably the last good surprise they'll have. My mom is all right, although she used to follow me around just like you're doing with Diana." She smiled. "She carried a switch, though. Life is tougher downstate."

"That's what I should have brought."

"Listen, the switch was just the opening act. Afterward she'd stand in the doorway of my room and listen to me wail. I'd say how sorry I was and how I was all done with it, and she'd just shake her head at me. She'd really get it going. Then she'd fly at me across that room, get right up in my face."

The girl leaned across the basin at me.

"Nose to nose," she said, "until I couldn't see anything but her. Then she'd say, 'Hope and regret. Hope and regret, child. You seem to be making a home for yourself exactly in between.'"

I smiled into the girl's face.

"That's good," I said.

She waved her hand and leaned back against the mirror. "My mom's all right. She's one old biddy."

She quieted when she said it, pressed her hands against her thighs, and then looked up at me.

"Well, I gotta go," she said.

Slowly, she slid off the countertop, then stopped.

"You know," she said, "there's a back door at the end of this hall. She won't even have to see you. Wouldn't that be a nice thing to do—to just sort of let her slowly realize you're gone?"

I shook my head at her.

"Well, I tried." She put out her hand. "Nice meeting you anyway."

I took her hand, so small it surprised me. "What's your name?" I asked her.

"Sharon."

"Sharon, she should come home with me."

She let go of my hand.

"Should and gonna," she said lightly. "Like my mama says."

Suddenly the door swung in and Diana stood there, holding it open, her face violently pale in the harsh light. She stared fiercely—first at the girl, then at me. No one said anything. From the darkened hallway behind her the din of the bar drifted in, and Sharon looked up, slipped past Diana, and was gone. Diana didn't move, one arm stiff to the door, her mouth a tight line. The pay telephone just outside the door began to ring, and I looked past her for a moment, thinking of my mother and Solomon's signal, of those shadowy rooms, the table still laid with picked-over plates, each of us now in these unlikely places. I lifted Diana's bottle from the counter, dropped it quietly in the trash, and looked at her.

"Let's go home now, OK?" I said.

She stood still. Her eyes flickered once when the ringing phone stopped. Then she turned and followed Sharon. The door swung shut behind her.

I drove home the long way, cutting down to the river again, then switching back randomly through the city. I passed the Kansas City Body Shop where my father had had our old Rambler serviced by two stiff and silent men who'd been deafened, he told me, by the same land mine. Farther on I saw Wonderland, a dingy, forbidden arcade where the city's bad boys had hung out when I was a child, and where once, in a quick surprise, my mother had taken Diana and me. It had been the weekend before New Year's Eve and we'd shopped all morning for our mother's party dress, pushing through thick crowds, me clutching the back of her coat, Diana clutching the back of mine. She decided on a red dress, a lovely dress—off the shoulder, cinched at the waist and falling into a long circle skirt that, she'd said, standing on tiptoe in the dressing room, would swirl lightly around her ankles when she danced. Afterward, out on the street again, she'd taken our hands suddenly, briskly, and led us into Wonderland, past boys slouched over pinball machines, boys rolling toothpicks in their mouths, to the front of the arcade, where she held her dress box in both hands and waited, smiling, while Diana and I each tried a quick draw with the life-sized mechanical outlaw in the window.

When I got to my mother's new building I pulled into the parking garage and drove to the lowest level, to the spaces reserved for visitors. It was dark down there, hollow with quiet after I shut off the car. I leaned back against the seat and sat still, closing my eyes. Perhaps they were up there, I thought, floors above me, my mother and sister, miraculously home, moving around the apartment in their nightclothes, my mother turning on the dishwasher and drawing the drapes, my sister leaning into the open refrigerator. I started suddenly and sat up in my seat, fumbling for my keys, one hand already on the door, propelled by the same huge hurry that had moved me mornings as a child whenever I woke to hear the sound of my family already at the breakfast table, their low voices and familiar rustlings drifting lightly up to my room as they began the day without me.

The Good Fight

Liza's friend, Dutton, had just told her he was convinced he was turning into a woman. After he said it, Liza looked up, confused. They were in a sports bar, a smoky, dark tunnel of a place festooned with pennants and jerseys tacked to the walls. She'd never been there before. After she picked Dutton up at O'Hare they'd taken the train into the city, found his hotel, and gone into the first bar they saw. She noticed that he ordered whiskey, which was new. Both Dutton's father and brother died alcoholics.

"What are you talking about?" she said. "What do you mean?"

"I mean I drive by her house at night. I drink coffee in the window of the corner restaurant near her work."

"Oh. You mean you're becoming a victim."

"Yes. Exactly."

"Well, that's depressing—to hear you think that's what a woman is."

"Sorry." He touched her hair, his fingers lingering at her temple. Then he leaned over to kiss her.

They had been friends for ten years, so his kiss quieted her. She stirred her drink, a gin drink, a summer drink—though it was a week past New Year's and bitter outside. When she looked up he was watching her.

"Maybe you are becoming a woman." She shook her head. "Men don't touch women like that anymore, you know, not good men, not with that kind of ease. They're frightened to death, I think, that their hand on a woman's arm, even at the small of her back, is too proprietary. Women, though, can touch anything. We've never owned anything. No one suspects we ever will."

Dutton watched her closely as she talked. She couldn't remember his ever being so attentive to her. It made her feel odd, guilty of something unnamed.

"I'm forty-three years old," he said. "Why is this happening to me?"

She didn't need to tell him why it was happening, because he knew. He was in love with a twenty-year-old girl—a tall, erotic blond named Serena. Earlier, on the train, he'd shown Liza her picture. "She's beautiful, isn't she?" he said.

She was. She was like a figurine, lean and muscled in a skimpy tank top, curled up next to a bare radiator. The radiator was white, her teeth were white, the sun shone through the undraped window behind her and made her hair glow white. Liza could see, though, the tension in her joints, in her knees and curled toes. Taut with self-consciousness her head inclined toward the camera to reveal the fine line of her cheekbone, she also revealed that for her surfaces mattered. This was a girl for whom illusion was a gift, like second sight.

Liza gave the picture back to him, and he slipped it into a compartment of a handsomely stitched and supple wallet. Dutton wore stylish clothes—razor-creased pleated pants, a loose linen shirt, and a thin, dark tie. He combed his hair, still thick and brown, straight back from his face which, though still handsome, told the truth: He was forty-three years old. He had grown too tired or wise to lie. This was what Liza admired most about Dutton. He did not lie anymore. He did not lie to women. Over the years, as their love rearranged itself into a kind of intimate friendship, Dutton had always been frank about a loneliness he had, a loneliness that sounded distinctly male, a loneliness eased only by wonderful women, he said, by making love with these women.

"You know," she said, "on the train when I saw Serena's picture I thought of what old men always say when they see a picture of some fresh young girl. They always say, 'Well, she's gonna break a lot of hearts,' and then everyone feels warm. But maybe what they mean is something more serious, you know, like what old generals must feel when they review enemy troop movements, that mixture of fear and hope for the good fight and then the disappointment of their own distance from it. Maybe that's what they mean."

"War."

"Maybe. I like to hope not, but probably I should give that up."

"I think so. For now, anyway. For awhile." He put his hand over hers and squeezed it because her husband was also in love with a twenty-year-old girl—a Japanese girl, new to this country—whom her husband met in the English as a Second Language class he taught. Liza had never seen her carefully posed in a photograph, but she had seen her in a courtroom, earlier that day, during the pretrial motions for Liza's and her husband's divorce. The girl sat quietly in the front row of the spectator section, her hands crossed over a tiny straw pocketbook in her lap—a small, delicate woman with eyes as dark as the inside of a chimney. When Liza saw her she was glad Dutton wasn't flying in until that night. It would have been a mistake for him to see her secrets this clearly. She wasn't sure she could bear to hear him speak honestly about them. Watching the girl, Liza believed no one should be allowed to witness divorce proceedings but the unhappy, fractious principals, all of whom looked equally drawn, humiliated, worse for the wear. Even the wives of rich men—women who walked to the bench with their heads high, chins jutted out, pursuing their entitlement—even they lingered a bit too long over their furs, folding them, patting them, sometimes stroking them during a long delay the way one would stroke a sleeping child.

In the courtroom Liza's husband fluttered between the Japanese girl and his lawyer. Once he stopped to crouch in front of the girl, to take her small hands in his, as he explained something to her. The girl did not speak. She seemed to communicate by lowering her eyes, parting her lips. She looked more aggrieved, more a victim, than any of the others in the courtroom, and Liza, watching her, felt rage throb in her throat and limbs. In that rage she felt huge, ungainly, American. She hardly felt like a woman at all, and that was a problem, she knew. Her attorney had told her to wear something feminine that day—something simple but pretty; no severe business suit, he'd said—because her husband had amended his petition. Her husband had decided that since he would soon be remarried, and since his future wife, unlike Liza, would be a full-time homemaker, he had grounds to pursue the sole legal custody of his and Liza's three-year-old daughter.

"Do you need to call about your child?" Dutton asked. He'd been watching her again.

"She's with them this weekend," Liza said, looking at her watch. "She's sleeping now." She arranged the folds of the dress she chose to wear that morning—a loose emerald green dress with a long, flowing skirt—and then she looked up at Dutton, noticing under his jaw the meticulous razor line that shaped his close-cut beard. "Dutton, I don't think I'm going to be able to sleep with you tonight."

He squeezed her hand again.

"Really," she said.

He let go of her hand but leaned closer to her. "You're talking too much, Liza. Terror makes you talk too much. You shouldn't. It makes up your mind before you do."

Liza looked away from him, out over the bar. This was an odd place for her to be. Near the door a ticker tape machine reported the latest sports scores. There were two televisions—one showing a car race, the other a basketball game—and scattered everywhere were backgammon and chess boards, men bent over them, squinting. Most of the patrons had gathered around a man throwing darts. Liza could tell by the man's face that he was a serious dart player and that he was losing. His mouth was firm and his eyes were clear but faraway, as if he were looking beyond the target to his fate. He reminded her suddenly of a boy named Bobby she loved in high school; a boy whose mother used to cry every night on the front stoop, a bottle of bourbon tucked between her ankles; a boy whose face nearly always looked like that.

"She doesn't talk at all," Liza said, looking back at Dutton. "He told me. She knows maybe thirteen words of English."

Dutton held up his empty glass to signal the waiter.

"Thirteen words, maybe twenty," Liza said. "Imagine. What could they be?"

"When I try to talk to Serena, she repeats whatever I say. I say, 'I love you,' and she says, 'You love me.' Sometimes it's a question. Sometimes it's a statement. Is that mystery or is that incoherence?"

"I'm not sure." Liza looked back to the dart player. "You're finding that out, I think." The player had finished his game. He took some folded bills out of a shot glass and slipped them into the shirt pocket of another man, then picked up a drink and walked to the back of the bar. "No. Forget I said that. She's twenty years old, Dutton. The only mystery is how much she doesn't know."

When Liza was twenty years old she didn't know anything. One day out of the blue Bobby showed up on her doorstep holding an embroidered poncho he'd brought back from Central America, where he had been in the Peace Corps. "I didn't know I was bringing this back for you," he told her. "But now I think that I was." She'd been intrigued and moved by the way those words sounded—so honest they frightened her. She made love to Bobby that night—something she'd been afraid to do when she was in love and in high school. That night, she was afraid not to. The foreign intricacy of sex made no sense to her, but she trusted him. She had, in her mind, the sound of him telling the truth. When it was over, he took her face in his hands. She knew he saw confusion. "You don't have to worry," he said. "This is important. This matters."

"You know, Dutton," she said now. "I've always been moved by the way people in love talk to each other. Haven't you? How can a man love a woman without language?"

"You're an abstract woman, that's why." He touched her hand again and smiled. "You talk too much, I told you that."

She smiled back at him. "A lot you know. You're in love with a woman who repeats whatever you say."

"In bed, Liza, people don't talk."

She took her hand out of his then and looked away from him. Suddenly tired, she wanted to go home. She wanted to find her daughter, carry her out to a cab, and ride the familiar road home. But that was impossible, and even if it were possible, it would not ease her. The familiar haunted her now—braiding her daughter's hair, stooping to tie her daughter's shoe. The more routine the gesture the more she was shaken by how deeply loss could touch her. That was why she asked Dutton to come, she realized, because he was not a part of her jeopardy. She wanted to believe her jeopardy had bounds, that there was some part of her life that could not be touched.

Dutton slid his chair next to hers and pulled her close, closer than they should have been in the front of a bar. She shut her eyes and felt him run his hand along the underside of her wrist. It was true; his touch did ease her. It eased her as much as anything he'd said tonight. Maybe that was what terror would teach her, that the language of feeling was unspoken, a language of gesture, of limbs and organs. She opened her eyes, looked at Dutton, and he stopped touching her. Then she knew that still she wanted him to say something.

"Maybe we should go back to the hotel. You've had a terrible day. You're tired. Sleep next to me, at least. I'll hold you. Someone should hold you."

"Not yet, no." She looked around the bar. Men were laughing, talking, leaning back in their chairs, as smooth and polished as a roomful of actors. "We should have dinner or something. There's a restaurant I know down the block."

He helped her on with her coat and they went. At the door he pulled her close again, under his arm. Outside the night was cold. Gusts of wind off the lake blew snow that had fallen that morning into their faces. They walked along the building to the end of the block. As they stepped away from its shelter at the corner a powerful wind hit them so hard that Liza stumbled on the step down to the street. Dutton caught her before she fell, but for a moment the ground swirled beneath her feet. She thought she might have to sit down on the curb. Next to her Dutton stood quietly in the cold, his hand under her elbow. She looked at him, and then he put his arms around her, pressed her head to his shoulder.

"I'm all right," she said into his ear. "Really I am. I'm glad you're here, Dutton."

He relaxed when she said it, then pulled her closer, and she thought, Words do ease us. They comfort us. Maybe they protect us in a way, rescue us from the agony of what our bodies feel.

Down the block the place Liza knew wasn't there anymore, and so they went into a Greek restaurant across the street—a loud, happy place, still decorated for the holidays with tinsel and hanging tissue-paper stars. A slight man with sleek, dark hair motioned them toward a cloakroom, then seated them in a corner booth near the bar.

Dutton ordered bread and cheese and a bottle of dry white wine, which Liza drank slowly. The place was still busy with a few large parties and crisscrossing waiters carrying plates of cheese, which they flamed at the table while the crowd shouted, "Opa!" Liza leaned into Dutton's shoulder and rested her head against the back of the booth. The wine warmed her. Dutton ate carefully, with one hand, so she wouldn't have to move. He brought a small forkful of cheese to her mouth, but she refused, shaking her head, raising her glass. She leaned deeper into his shoulder and looked across the restaurant at a young girl, maybe eleven or twelve, with shining hair and eyes. When the waiter brought a platter of cheese, her parents and two elderly women and a little boy who might have been her brother sang "Happy Birthday" to her. Other diners turned, the girl smiled, and the waiter lighted their cheese with a flourish, holding it high above the table for an instant like a blessing.

In the next moment, the tissue-paper star above the family was on fire. One of the elderly women gave out a shrill cry, and the young girl looked at her in horror, unaware of the fire over her head. Her father swept her out of her chair and toward the front door just as pieces of glowing ash fluttered down on their table. Most of the diners stood silently, holding their napkins. A few backed away from a small trail of flame that traveled the room along a crepe-paper streamer. Dutton took Liza's glass out of her hand, but they sat still in their booth as the waiter who had lighted the cheese stood on the girl's empty chair, batted the star to the ground, and stomped on it. Across the room, another waiter did the same with the crepe-paper streamer. The slight man who had met Liza and Dutton at the door appeared from the kitchen holding a fire extinguisher. He smiled when he saw what the waiters had done.

"Opa!" he said, raising the extinguisher. "Opa!"

The crowd of diners hesitated a moment, then began to applaud. Next to Dutton, Liza began to cry.

"Here," Dutton whispered, taking her hand, drawing her to her feet. "Come here." He steered her between tables into the alcove full of coats, pushed past a rack of them to a private corner. "Here," he said again. He handed her his handkerchief, but she wasn't crying now, her tears replaced by a deep, sorrowful exhaustion. She leaned against an emergency exit and felt the weather outside, stony and cold against her back. In the dark of the alcove she couldn't see Dutton's expression, but she knew he was watching her again with that acute attention. She was frightening him. She should say something. Before she could he moved closer, pressed against her, his warmth and yielding weight a strange contradiction to the steel door behind her. He touched her chin, pushed her hair behind her ear. She felt his breath, light and alert, on her neck. He drew his hands down her shoulders to her elbows and wrists and then to her waist, where he held her. She felt then what Dutton had been talking about all those years. She felt the exact relief of his hands. Every place he touched became a place where her sorrow was not. For a moment, she was happy. She put her arms around him. As she leaned into him, away from the door, she felt his loneliness, too. In the curve of his chest she felt herself occupying its space. Staring over his shoulder she knew also, suddenly and sadly, that it would return, unchanged, her sorrow, his loneliness. This was only one moment. What she was learning under his hands was not the kind of knowledge that formed a path in the mind; it wouldn't lead her anywhere.

She stared over his shoulder at the darkest corner of the alcove, at the two walls and the shadow of their juncture. "I love you, Dutton," she said suddenly. When she said it she didn't know why she was saying it, or even if she was lying, but he pulled her closer, he clutched her, and she realized that the longing for a woman to speak these words to him had provoked much of his life, and now, at least, he had heard them.

Everyone
Is Wearing
a Hat

When my husband comes to bed I am already there, reading a popular magazine. He climbs in heavily beside me, jouncing the mattress, and says, "Get the light, will you, hon?" Even when we are alone together my husband talks too loud.

"Why do you do that?"

"What?"

"Shout. I'm right here next to you."

He pulls himself up on one elbow and smiles at me. "Then why is the light still on?"

I look back at the magazine. "In just one minute. In one more paragraph, okay?"

He doesn't say anything. Instead, he rocks his head on his pillow, folds his hands over his stomach, makes his face a cartoon of patience. My husband is a large man—dark, meaty, barrel-chested, with the blue sheen of his beard always showing at his jaw, a thatch of black hair that stands up from his forehead. Even when he is dressed and serious he looks exaggerated, like a caricature of a man, like the brute in a children's story, and this pains me. When we were younger he had a lovely habit, at crosswalks and in open doorways, of resting one hand just under my shoulderblades with the gentle pressure of a dance. I'd glance furtively at him, believing his spirit was as lithe and arresting and keen as the weight of his hand, and I'd mourn the cruel irony of his broad looks. Now he crosses his ankles and sighs as he smooths the bedcover over his chest.

"I get you. I get you," I say, reaching behind me to turn out the light.

We lie there in the dark, tossing lightly to find our shapes in the mattress. Then he says, quieter now, "What was that all about?"

I sit up in bed again. Lately I find myself giving up my own comfort for the chance to tell my husband something new.

"It was an article about dreams and men and women," I tell him. "It said women laugh more in their dreams than men do." I pause a moment to allow him to make up his mind. Then I say, "Now what is that supposed to mean?"

I'm suddenly interested again in what things mean. For a long time, I wasn't. I did take our son Nathaniel—Natty—to museums and river caverns, and one year to see a mossy replica of the dank cabin, the crude bed and furnishings, that marked the beginning of Abraham Lincoln's stingy, melancholy life. But then I was more concerned with what all those things meant to Natty—a thin, excitable, open-mouthed sort of boy, with pale blond hair, pale skin, almost translucent. Outside Lincoln's timber doorway or packed into a tour shuffling dimly through Steamboat Cave, in the presence of any huge mystery, Natty opened one eye wider than the other and stiffened with expectation. Seeing him like that I always felt compelled to smooth his hair or shoulders, and I forgot myself.

Nine months ago, when he was eight, Natty was crossing Hinkson Avenue when he was killed by a man driving a burgundy late-model pickup truck with a license plate that began EXK or JXK or J8E. Witnesses gave the police these details, and so that is what the police gave us. They have not found the truck or the man.

Just before the funeral I touched Natty's hand, fingering a familiar crescent-shaped nick on his thumb where he had closed a door on it. Yearning filled my chest like a bright light. I've met my loss, I thought. Kneeling beside him I closed my eyes and pressed his hand to my face. I knelt that way until my husband squeezed my shoulder. "Natty's gone," he said, drawing Natty's hand away from me. I stared up at him. His fingers dug sharply into the flesh of my shoulder. His face was strangely, unaccountably firm.

"What is it?" I asked.

He drew me solidly to my feet. There was no question in his touch, not a doubt. He led me through a doorway and into a small anteroom hushed with long shadows. We stood in front of a draped window. Outside it was early evening. Through the window I saw a darkening path lined with purple phlox, blooms as heavy and round as a child's head. We stood quietly a moment, my husband's hand still on my shoulder. "Natty's gone now," he said again.

I knew that. I knew Natty was gone, but with his hand pressed to my cheek, his body still held a power, one final intimacy. That is what I had wanted to mourn—the loss of his touch, his weight, the small light bones that had grown and passed through my own body. Once, as a girl, under the flowered daybed in our family room, I'd watched in horror as my calico cat devoured her own kitten—a tiny, crooked, limp thing, born dead. At that window, our son's body a room away, I understood the impossible estrangement I'd witnessed then. Slowly, I reached up to take my husband's hand from my shoulder, and after I'd held it a moment, I squeezed, hard, until I was certain I'd hurt him. Then I walked out into the funeral garden.

I sat alone on a small bench in the garden I'd seen through the window. The bouquets of purple phlox hung heavy on their slender stalks. Scattered among them, orange day lilies had already closed for evening. A bed of yellow and pink pansies shimmered at the bank of a round reflecting pool. The path I'd seen was decorative. It led back to a stockade fence grown over with ivy, and stopped. This was a formal garden. Someone had planned it for effect—to soothe me, to simplify my grief in a sentimental setting of lush and redolent growth, with the murmur of water, that small winding path. Even I was part of the design. I stood up quickly. I was the person for whom the bench had been planned.

That moment, my standing alone in the darkened garden, stricken with loss and sudden self-consciousness, is how Natty's death continues to happen to me. Life, no longer ordinary, becomes profligate—a reckless boil of mute, mystifying details. This morning, before dawn, a tree moved in the wind outside, its branches rattling the window like a handful of marbles. I bolted out of sleep and sat rigid, drawing the sheet around me, listening in the dark. Last week, in an elevator, rocketing to the twenty-sixth floor and my dentist's office downtown, I stood breathless and blinking, having just realized, like some character in a parable stunned into sensibility, that everyone but me was wearing a hat.

My husband turns to me now and says, "What did the article say the difference meant?"

I slide back down in bed. "Well, it doesn't," I say. "It makes a sort of feeble attempt to link it to hormones or something—says a dreaming woman suffers giddy bursts of estrogen—but it backs off even from that."

"Huh," my husband says. He is being kind now. I haven't told him enough to impress him. He is punching his pillow. He is thinking of rest. "Didn't Lulu used to laugh in her sleep?"

Lulu was a black cocker spaniel we had for the first six years we were married. She slept constantly, like an old cat, sometimes fifteen, twenty hours a day, and the only way I had to judge her affection was where she chose to nap. In the beginning she liked the head of our bed, where she'd bury her muzzle under my husband's pillow. Then, for a year or so, she moved to the bottom of my closet, among my shoes. Finally she ended up in Natty's room, in the small space of bare floor between his headboard and the wall. Nothing I ever noticed accounted for these changes, but now, when I think of her, I think, "Lulu. First she was my husband's dog, then she was mine, and then she was Natty's."

"Lulu *ran* in her sleep," I tell my husband. "She'd pant and move her legs." I paddle my arms to show him.

"Ha," my husband says. "That's right." He turns to look at me as he remembers, and I feel his breath warm on my cheek. "Where was that animal going?"

"Who knows." We smile then, together, in the dark.

"Well," he says and draws me against him.

We lie that way awhile, back to front, breathing, listening. The house is warm this evening. Earlier, it rained buckets, a sudden twilight storm that flew against the house in roars, then stopped. It's spring again. One of us should open a window. Thinking about it I am suddenly not sleepy. I could get up, make a cup of coffee, sit on the back porch, maybe walk in the yard, wait for the moon. I don't know what I want to do. My husband's chest falls, then rises against my back. I am keeping him awake, I know.

"I'm sorry," I say. "I need to make up my mind—sleep or get up."

"I'm fine," he tells me and presses closer, drawing his knees up behind mine. We could make love, I think, and then realize that is what he has just told me. I am oddly, deeply embarrassed not to have understood that immediately. Although I mean to press lightly against him, in my response I move too quickly, in a strange brief spasm. My ankle catches his shin sharply, and then I freeze like a hapless girl, too mortified even to apologize. My throat and eyes fill suddenly with tears, but I lie there still as a stone, watch the digital clock change, 29 to 30, and wonder at how a sorrow so much larger than this moment can be so neatly contained by it.

My husband is quiet behind me, his breathing shallow and alert. Then he draws the sheet up over our shoulders, tucks a corner under my hair. "I don't think dogs laugh," he says. "Don't they just smile sometimes?"

"You should throw me out of bed," I tell him. "Put your foot between my shoulders and shove."

"Oh," he says. "Well."

I roll over in his arms, see that he is wide awake and watching me, then I roll back. We both settle deeper into the bed, press against each other again.

"There should be a book or something to look these things up in." He yawns. I feel him relax again. "An Encyclopedia of Dog Lore," he says.

"There probably is one. It's probably on someone's coffee table right now—next to the Herbal Guide to Ending Human Misery." I turn to lie on my back, pull my arms up behind my head, then take them down again. "What I would want explained," I say, "about the dogs, I mean, is why they would do one and not the other—just smile, never laugh." I look at him. "Assuming they were capable."

He thinks this over. "Bemused but not amused, huh? Maybe that's it. Decorum. Maybe they always feel like guests." He likes this idea. He draws his pillow under his neck. I see his teeth flash in the dark. "Sure, it's our house," he says, "our sofa. We get to pick the dog food and which TV shows to watch. They don't even know the language. They're like those tour groups of Chinese businessmen you see on the news, standing at a baseball game, holding a hot Polish and a beer. Sure. Laughing would be un-seemly, just too cocky, as if they knew what was what."

He is having a good time, even giggling a little, as if we were drunk or young. I listen to him and think, "This isn't what I wanted to talk about." I don't know what it is I do want to talk about.

"Lulu never felt like a guest," I tell him.

He doesn't say anything.

"She was part of the family."

"Hey," he says. "Hey."

We are both quiet then. The bed is still. The room is still. My skin draws tight with the silence. Outside a car goes by and I wish I were in it, or that I were a tree, or the ground, absorbing all that rain.

"Come here," he says.

I don't want to—his voice is too harsh in the quiet room—but I do. "What?"

He gropes, finds my face in the dark, and holds it between his hands for a moment.

"What?" I say again.

He kisses me. For a moment I lie there and let him, relieved that this is all he wants. Often these days he seems too large or loud, his hands too heavy, and I don't want him to touch me—or I do, but in a way he doesn't know. A week ago I rolled away from him when I woke to see him staring at me, cradling one of my palms against his cheek. Later that afternoon he went out to help a neighbor trim a diseased elm, and from the window I watched him hanging from the thickest branch, swaying lightly in a sling of slender rope as he struggled with the long-handled saw. He leaned back dangerously to set the blade, and when he shook his hair to clear his vision sweat flew off in a ringed mist. I wanted him then, but only then, for that one moment, that one gesture, shaking his head in the sun, defying gravity. I feel him waiting now, so I put my arms around him.

"There," he says. "Now come close and settle in, will you?"

I do what he says, draw close to his side, press my cheek to his large chest. Quickly, he is nearly asleep. His body loosens and uncurls from mine. When I feel his hand open on my shoulder and slip away I press my cheek harder against his chest. "Why were we talking about that?" I say.

"You were reading about women and men, about the different sounds they make when they're dreaming." He answers me without stirring, his voice low and colorless, as though he were already sleeping, as though he were talking in his own dream. I feel his body weighty and warm next to mine. On the crown of my head even his breath is warm.

"Oh," I say. I lean back to look at him, see that his eyes are closed, his face is slack, his jaw slightly agape. "The thing is," I say. He opens his eyes, looks at me gravely, but I go on. "I still don't understand what it means. It must mean something or it wouldn't happen."

"Maybe," he says, closing his eyes again, pressing my cheek to his chest with one wide hand. "Maybe it's just a fact."

I lie there a moment. I want to be soothed by what he's said. I understand that facts comfort him, that like the men in that magazine, he is different, and difference is all he has to offer. His hand slips away from me. He is sleeping now. Under my cheek there is the sturdy rhythm of his heart and breath, and as fact that, too, should comfort me, but it does not. Slowly, I slide away from him, to the far side of the bed, where I sit up and watch him, a darker shadow in the dark. His chest shudders once and he sprawls into a deeper sleep, throwing one arm over my thigh, his breath a loud string of rattling snores. His arm is heavy, a wooden dead weight on my thigh. Suddenly I kick it off me, wanting to wake him, to tell him he is wrong, deluded by his own thick body, by the warm wide circle of his arms and the comfort he believes waits for me there. I want to tell him the whole surface of his life is a fraud, that inside even his literal, loutish sleep, some terrible provocation throbs.

In the breeze outside the tree taps the window again and draws me out of bed in the dark. The sheet slides soundlessly to the floor as I stand there, and briefly, in a pale flash, I think of Natty, of my pale child, of his face, still smooth and credulous, as he glanced up to see . . . what? The silver grille of a burgundy truck? A license plate that began EXK or JXK or J8E? There wouldn't have been time for his mind to name it—only the dark roar of mystery, and him there, poised, one eye wider than the other, open-mouthed and alone, a moment just shy of the blow that would end all he'd known as fact.

Real Love

Like lots of Americans, Nin looked for real love
and found mainly where it wasn't. It wasn't on TV. It wasn't at
the movies. Hardly any singers sang about it in songs. She had
not yet found it in the locus of experience that after she was dead
would be called her life.

In that plight she felt citizenship in something larger than herself. One of her faults was thinking other people were like her,
that men on elevated trains, staring blankly at their own reflections in the tinted window, actually sat sifting through the mys-
terious confluence of their pasts, presents, and futures while they
wondered, *Where is my real love?* Sure, she knew imagining mu-
tuality most often marked an imposition of ego, but it comforted

her. Wasn't that why, she reasoned, people constructed the sweet myths of state and country. And what about that national anthem, one song for many voices, posing its own string of unanswered questions. *Have you seen my flag?* it asked. *Oh say, can you see it?* Nin felt certain that in the heart those questions lived no more than a gentle remove from *Where is my real love?*

Then one day she decided—after seven years alone; seven years raising a child in apartments with bugs and bad light and poor heat; seven years living inside herself like a potted plant, always equally aware of both desire and constraint—to go to Arizona. In order to get there, she told a lie. She parked her dear son and two weeks of summer shorts, tee-shirts, and underwear at his father's place, and to his father, her long-standing ex-husband, Nin said, "I need some time alone, a new geography, one with peaks to stun me, loosen whatever I've been clutching. When that happens," she said, "I'll be right back. Honest."

She believed the lie when she told it, stood a little more erect with this false proclamation of personal need, but she was going off, really, to meet a man, an older man named William McKinley, like the mountain and dead president. The name suited him. He was craggy, accomplished, steady, and at least two full shades more conservative than Nin, which meant he believed in age and was therefore made uneasy by the difference twenty-three years created in his mind between him and her. At a restaurant the night he asked her to go to Arizona, Nin watched him notice the waiter calculating her youth, and she saw something—it might have been fear—register in long lines on his face, but still he reached for her, the grave pressure of his hand on her own implying that he risked everything, his power and authority, the long line of days and nights with which he had built his accomplishment, all of it somehow called up and in jeopardy during the few moments he awaited her response. She wasn't sure anyone had ever taken her so seriously.

Nin risked only the lie to her son's father, a man who during the years they'd been married told lies of such baroque magnificence that she felt moved to explain long-distance to her sister, who believed Nin stood on the verge of a huge mistake, just why her own lie was okay.

"Listen," Nin said. "I could lie to that man every day until I died, and still we would not be even."

"True," her sister said. "Well, sort of." She was younger than Nin, which meant Nin had sat through years of similar awful pauses in their conversations, during which Nin always imagined her sister making mental notes, adding chapters to her private manual of self-help, which was How To Avoid Nin's Mistakes, Nin's Pain, Nin's Circumstances, Nin's Consequences. Still, they were sisters, blood, and so Nin offered up her life as a cautionary gift, which her sister accepted hesitantly, like a collect call.

"Actually, he only told you one lie, the same lie," her sister said. "He just told it a lot of ways."

That lie had been banal, predictable: that he loved Nin when he didn't; that the clerical girl who hung around his office until past 11 P.M. was only using the computer to finish up her undergraduate thesis on Henry James; that she was simply a sweet, serious, well-meaning girl who needed a computer; and no, of course he had never touched her, had never thought of touching her.

———————

"You have to believe me," he called late one night from the office to say. "Who would think of touching a girl so devoted to scholarship, to Henry James, no less? You're misapprehending some chaste scholarly business here."

Nin believed differently. She believed that as her husband delivered that speech he reached out to smooth a flyaway hair behind the girl's ear, his hand lingering at the tender nape of her neck. Her own body, stationed at the other end of the phone, registered on a cellular level the concussion of that touch, which delivered to her two certainties: one, an abiding belief in the extrasensory; and two, her husband was already gone. Years and thousands of dollars of attorney fees later, Nin found out she'd been right, and occasionally now, because she was finally only months shy of paying off the debt, she and her sister joked about how expensive it was to find out she'd been right about exactly two things.

"Go if you have to," her sister said. "Though I think you might get where you're going faster if you just jumped off your roof."

In Arizona, motoring the mountain switchbacks and narrow passes in William's steel gray rental car, Nin remarked on the landscape.

"Wow," she said. "Magnificent. Incredible. Big."

Comfortable with being struck dumb, she felt small but tucked into some slot of the world. Not sure where they were going, she enjoyed the ride, and they weren't bothering a soul, for miles passing only trees and rocks and an occasional meadow of wildflowers.

Outside the town where he'd rented a place an elk ranch ran along both sides of the road, and Nin peered into the tangle of downed branches, tall grasses, and pine forest, looking for a massive head, a haunch, a whisper of motion. She'd never seen an elk, but felt certain she'd recognize one, and, pleased by the idea of an animal so distinctive, she suddenly saw everything for what it was. A tree was just bark and branches and leaves, a flower a dot of color on a field of green, and she was a lonely woman sitting next to a good, quiet man, who grew more quiet as he slowed for the town, moving his hand briefly from the gear shift to Nin's knee as if to quiet her, too, before he turned onto the gravel lane that wound back to the place he'd rented. Seeing it, a square wooden house with a blue door, Nin thought, Well, here I am, somewhere else.

The first day she and William hiked what looked like a horse trail leading up out of the canyon of town. Maneuvering narrow, dusty paths along a wall of red rock, Nin discovered hiking was different from the walking she did back home along the lakefront in the city. Hiking was up and down and over and around, requiring the tiny stutter steps of a marine. Because Nin lacked a marine's respect for what was possible and what was not, she gave in to the urge to step out to full stride, a lapse that led quickly to grave lightheadedness. Fearful she would faint, topple down the wall of rock and die, she stopped at a clearing to breathe thin air in through her mouth.

"How far have we gone?" she asked, though they weren't headed anywhere in particular. There was nothing they'd set out to see at the end of any of these trails. Nin wasn't even sure these trails ended. They might wind on forever, up one mountain, then down again and up another. Or maybe they all converged somewhere, and from that spot spread out in a web of blind alleys intended to distract a person from the true path, like the coloring-book mazes her boy traced his way through at home. Nin knew this place wasn't wilderness—wilderness would be unmarked by any trail—but it was closer to wilderness than she'd ever been, and she wasn't sure how it all worked, who made these paths, and what those people were after or where they meant to end up.

They'd hiked since dawn and it was nearly eleven, but William said they'd come just under two miles, information that sat Nin down hard against a dead tree that still stood upright, a few curled leaves shivering in its branches. Peeling off layers of clothing that had brought her through the chill of the morning, Nin said, "I'll just rest a minute. Just one minute," but she arranged the clothing into a kind of pallet, as if she meant to sleep there.

William didn't say anything, offered her water wordlessly, and she accepted that silence as proof of his wisdom and good character. It allowed her to close her eyes comfortably, retreat into herself for reserves.

Inside the dark of her head the web of paths led her to the word *fractal*, which she'd learned at her son's curriculum night just before she left. Her son's science teacher, a young man, fresh and eager and determined to be understood, had used it to explain the shoreline of Lake Michigan, which he claimed to be endless and immeasurable—each inlet, he said, internally complicated by countless other inlets, down and down in scale to the microscopic and beyond. He told the parents that even if they could straighten the shoreline out, pull it like a thread and lay it flat, they'd never know its true length because they'd never stop pulling. Each inlet contained countless more, one inside the other. "You simply can't know it," is how he ended.

Nin had worried like a Republican over her child's fate in that young man's hands, imagining her son's golden promise and sweet disposition unraveling as he galloped after mystery. Later she decided maybe it was okay to include in a child's education those things that he could never know. Maybe it would save her own child time and trouble. Decades of time, she thought now, leaning against the wobbly tree trunk. Truckloads of trouble. Suddenly she reached out for William.

"Oh," she said, frightened by her own sadness. "I'm so tired."

He moved closer then, and put his arms around her. As his hands moved over her light tee-shirt and then beneath it to her skin, he said her name. She wondered if he meant to make love to her there in the dirt. Last night, in the privacy of the rented cabin, he couldn't. With alternating tenderness and fury he touched her, but he could not make love, and he ended in a tangle next to her, the sound of his breath moist in her ear, both of them unable to call up words, stilled by passion so close and impossible to enter.

Late into the night he got up, dressed, and left. Nin heard his rental car start and crunch down the gravel lane. At the window, the floor icy beneath her bare feet, she watched his headlights turn onto the highway away from town and realized she didn't love him. No terrible wound opened as he drove off; no fear for her or his future stood next to her, just benign concern. He was her friend, and she hoped he'd be okay out there. In the city he might only have needed a walk around the block to find proof that people like them belonged in the world. The city was thick with people who temporarily couldn't say or do either what they meant or didn't mean. Out here he would probably have to go farther, and he'd have to pass the shadows of all those elk.

Some time later his key in the door woke her, and Nin lay blinking in the dark as he moved through the house. He stopped in the kitchen for what Nin hoped was whiskey, then came to stand next to the bed.

From the shadows, he said, "I'm sixty years old and frightened as a school boy. That's what you're seeing here."

Then he stripped naked and crawled in next to her. She liked the way he settled in, pulling the pillow under his neck, folding the bedcovers over his narrow chest, resigned to himself. She appreciated, then, what age did to men, chastening them, drawing lines through their fine features, stealing their potency, forcing them to see what else they might be, besides a man, and she felt tempted to resign herself to him, offer him her life and attention and devotion, even though he was her friend and not her real love. But how could she explain that to him, and even if she could, hadn't he survived enough knowledge for one night.

Nin was pretty certain he didn't sleep, but she did, waking from time to time to experience his silence, his stillness next to her an embodiment of deep thought. Once she took his hand, drew it under her chin, and felt herself drawn more intimately into the circle of his consideration. She slept that way until morning.

Now, in the dirt, she took his hand again, and they lay back against the ground, the sun high in the sky above them. After a time, he said, "There's a town with a bar less than an hour's walk away. I could carry you if I had to."

They made it in just over an hour. Lightened by the idea of a destination, they told stories along the way, and at the bar they remained light, drinking cold beers in their dirty hiking clothes, leaning over to watch the woman bartender trace the easiest route home on their map. She was a great-looking woman in canvas trousers and a flannel shirt who had moved up there with her horse from Albuquerque. Before that, she'd lived in Bozeman and for a while outside of Taos, but this was the best place she'd been, she said. Even her horse, who'd always been skittish, calmed down. When their chicken sandwiches were ready at the window of a kitchen in back, William left the bar to pick them up. Both Nin and the bartender watched him go. Then they turned back to each other. The woman's face, dark and lined from living so close to the sun, bobbed in front of Nin's as she washed glasses.

"You guys in love?" she said.

Either the question or how easily she pronounced the word *love* startled Nin.

"I don't know." Nin looked over her shoulder. William stood just outside the bright light spilling from the kitchen window. Even in shadow he looked exactly like the man he was—tall, sharp-shouldered, decent.

The woman dried her hands slowly on her apron, then tapped one cigarette from a pack she'd sold Nin earlier.

"Do you mind?"

Nin shook her head.

The woman snapped off the filter, rolled the cigarette between her fingers, and then lit it, inhaling deeply. She blew a stream of smoke from the corner of her mouth and smiled.

"It looks like love to me," she said.

"I know," Nin said. "It does, doesn't it?"

The Next Day

Tonight it is my wife's idea to get a dog. She reaches over in the dark, takes the cigarette out of my mouth, puts it in hers and says, "Tucker, all my life I wanted one. When I used to pray, that's what I'd pray for. I remember one birthday I walked home real slow from school, dragged my feet and thought, 'They'll open that door and a little dog will come running out.'"

"That's from a movie," I say. "What movie is that from?"

"A parakeet," she tells me, inhaling deeply. "That's what they got me. I never even liked the thing, and then something happened to its head, like a wound or an abscess that kept spreading. I'd tell my father every morning at breakfast, 'That bird is dying,'

I'd say, 'It makes odd noises,' and my father would say, 'You just don't feed it enough.' So I fed it more and it got fatter, but the wound kept spreading until one day I came home from school and the room was stone quiet. I didn't even want to look. I just stood in the doorway and tried to stare past its cage and right into the next day."

We are in bed when she tells me this. Often, especially since I've been out of work, Joan and I lie in bed, smoke cigarettes in the dark, and she tells me stories about herself as a girl, sometimes until two or three in the morning. She has to be at the bank by eight, but we are newly married. In the glow of our cigarettes and the streetlight outside the window, our faces are yellow, pink and intent. Our lowered voices in the dark are a promise.

Joan glances at me to see if I am still listening.

"It died, didn't it?" I say, touching her lip as I reach for the cigarette.

"Yeah," she says. Leaning back, she folds her hair over the headboard, then sits up again. "They made me bury it myself. Oh, I thought of just dropping it in the trash burner, but I took it out to an empty lot behind the house and even made a little cross out of sticks. The ground was so hard I broke blood vessels in my hands digging. All this blood welled up in pools under my palms but wouldn't break through. I remember being confused by that."

"It's the same thing as a bruise, I think."

"I was young," she says. "And it didn't look like a bruise." She holds her palms in front of her face. "I was only nine, and it looked more serious than that."

She stares past her hands, past me, over my shoulder, when she says it, as though she can just make out a younger outline of herself leaning there against the dark. I turn and stare with her, though I don't see anything. My wife's voice in the dark has an absolute authority.

I think I know what she sees, though. As a girl Joan was always too tall and skinny and awkward-looking. Her neck was very long, and, sitting on top of it, her head appeared a little unbalanced. Joan is one of those women who grew up not liking the way she looked. I see it in the way she holds her body in old snapshots—sort of tense and willing herself backward, a stance of total dissatisfaction, almost as if she'd asked to be the tree she's standing under and hasn't forgotten, hasn't come to terms with, the mix-up.

When most girls' faces were soft and round, with tiny noses and pink patches at the cheeks, like the faces you see in Fourth of July photographs or soft-drink commercials, Joan's was long, angular and dark, with jutting cheekbones, a strong jaw, and full, ruddy lips. At thirteen she was five feet eight, and in her class picture from that year, her face, huge with color and angle, rises out of a group of pale, plump eighth graders, all of whom appear utterly eager, absolutely wholesome. Above them all is Joan, frowning, angry, daring you to notice that she is the only girl in the back row or that the nun, a tight-lipped guardian angel, is standing behind her on a riser, hands placed firmly on Joan's shoulders, as if to keep her from growing right through the ceiling.

As a woman Joan has grown into her face, though it remains striking and strange. Sometimes, especially in the evening when she is tired and sitting down to supper with her coffee, her face softens, eases into such a compelling pose that I can never fully concentrate on anything else. Patient and faraway, she measures her sugar, lets it fill and run off her spoon twice. She stirs her coffee lightly, and then, resting her chin on one hand, she looks at me with a face so womanly and frank that I am embarrassed and filled with hope.

We eat supper quietly, passing plates, slicing pats of butter. Afterward, we stand at the sink together, and in the steamed kitchen window I watch our reflections to see if she is tired and warm enough to accept my admiration. If she is, we go to bed, and later she tells me stories about herself and I am proud. I believe she tells me these stories because she trusts me to love her more than she loves herself. This is how people merge, I think.

Days, especially mornings, she is different—taut, guarded, again the girl in that class picture—so rigidly composed that sometimes I worry her body might be secretly plotting rebellion, growing furtive tumors, ulcers, cancers, caching away reserves of thwarted energy to turn against her one day in a sudden convulsion or hemorrhage. Maybe because I'm older than Joan—twenty-nine and looking at thirty—or maybe because I can't find work, I am a man with an inkling of terror. I am certain that anything can happen to anyone. So I try to get her to relax.

The only even slightly recreational thing she does is a little oil painting, and that takes from her more than it gives. She'll squint, lean back from her easel and freeze, stony with concentration. I give her back rubs and lectures on the benefits of exercise. Once I even brought up meditation. First she ignored me, and then she got angry.

"Just stop looking at me if it makes you so morbid," she told me.

But I can't stop looking. That much tension in a woman's body, in my own wife's body, makes me afraid even to tiptoe across the room. One morning she caught me staring at her while she made orange juice. She likes to squeeze it fresh, and this particular morning I was amazed by the strain I saw in her neck and shoulders. Each time she pressed an orange half to the juicer the tendons in her neck stood out and the muscles in her back rolled under the thin straps of her nightgown. She looked like a horse pulling a plow. She had just glanced over her shoulder to say something pleasant—I could see it in her eyes waiting to be said—when she caught me in a whole-body stare. I think even my mouth was open. I tried to look away, as though the can opener had drawn my attention, but I saw her eyes empty and then fill up.

"You know," she said in a voice that sounded moist, like she had tears far back in her throat. "If I were a pot, I'd crack."

Then she threw the oranges, juice, and juicer into the sink and walked out, but as she swept past, all legs and arms and neck in her short gown, I could tell she didn't want to walk out of the room so much as just disappear.

Tonight, though, Joan relaxes on two stacked pillows, drapes one leg over mine and decides she wants a Scottish terrier because they can be dignified and comic simultaneously, and because of one that an old lady brings into the bank with her.

"She makes him wear this ridiculous plaid jacket," she tells me. "Normally I hate dogs in coats, but with this one I can tell he's embarrassed and trying to make the best of it. I think he's even embarrassed by the old woman."

She stubs out the cigarette and draws the sheet lightly over us. I lie next to her in the dark and decide to look for a Scottish terrier. I decide to stop making cabinets, which is what I do when I'm out of work, and make calls to every kennel in the four-state area.

The cheapest Scottish terrier I find is six years old and costs $550. Puppies go for $750. I've been out of work for nine weeks and sold one cabinet to my second cousin, so Joan and I drive out into the country early one Saturday morning and pick the runt of a litter of shepherd/collie mix out of what looks like an old horse trough.

"That one," Joan says, and she looks good saying it. She doesn't try to hide that her face is announcing this is the puppy she'd waited for that birthday afternoon. I am proud of her. I think, "This is my wife and this is our dog and now I will drive us all home." We've only been married eight months, but already in my mind the words, *wife, husband, marriage,* toll with tradition and reputation.

She decides to call him "Larry Hochstetler" after the little farm kid with dirty hands and hair who lifts him from the trough to her arms. Immediately, Larry seems a frightened but adaptable puppy. He squeals when he is taken from his mother, then rests his muzzle on the slope of Joan's neck and shoulder, closes his eyes. I want to beam at her, standing there nuzzling the puppy in a rectangle of light that falls through the doorway of the shed. She looks warm and young and still a little sleepy around the eyes. Instead, I trace crosshatch lines in the dirt floor with the toe of my shoe. The farm kid pats Larry's rump twice, and Joan reaches out to run her hand through the kid's hair so that it stands up spiky and surprised. His mother, who had met us at the car and led us down a steep hill looking straight, full-breasted, and strong in a sleeveless yellow dress and rough shoes, pulls her arms around her waist and smiles.

I watch Joan's face over the dog's ears, and when she looks over them, thanking me with her eyes, I take my hands out of my pockets and step forward too quickly, as if I were falling.

When Joan sees this she stops smiling, hikes Larry farther up on her shoulder and sends the mother a familiar glance. Both women's expressions change to something humorous, tolerant.

"We'd best go," Joan says. "This moment is getting a little ripe."

Saturday nights are quiet at our house. We open the windows if it's warm, turn off most of the lights, and do separate things. I lie on the sofa watching television and circling want ads while Joan works at her easel in the corner. Larry moves between her feet and mine, sometimes stopping at the bed I built him to tear at an old knotted knee sock of Joan's. We have had him seven weeks, and now we are in the chewing stage. He really is a good puppy. He house-trained with ease and spends most of the day outside on a long piece of rope tied to the porch railing, frisking in the yard or just stretched across the front stoop, taking the sun.

Afternoons, I work with him on obedience, and he already understands Come, Sit, and Stay, which Joan says is enough. She says what we need is a civilized dog, not a vaudevillian, and she is probably right. I know she was right to decide we needed a dog. Before Larry, even on random, ordinary nights like this one, there remained a precise, odd distance between us. I remember one morning, lying in bed, I opened my eyes directly on Joan's face. She was still asleep, so close to me I could have pursed my lips and kissed her, when I had one of those peculiar, half-coherent morning thoughts.

"That is the edge of her," I thought, "and this is the edge of me."

But Larry nudges himself into that space, gives us something to be gentle with and afraid for, that isn't each other. Some nights he'll nose his way up from the foot of the bed to bury his muzzle between Joan's pillow and mine. Over his head, we smile at each other.

"What are you watching?" Joan asks. Her easel sits in the far corner of the living room, and I have to raise my shoulders to see her. She has pulled her hair up on top of her head and has a jointed lamp clipped to the windowsill behind her, directed at the canvas. The bright light catches a ring of fine hair that has fallen at her ears and neck and makes it a mist.

"It's about an older woman having her first baby," I tell her. "She's forty-four or something. I'm not really watching it."

"You know, the other day I was eating lunch in that park across from the bank, and I saw this nice older couple." She looks over her canvas at me. "They were ordinary people, I don't know, in their fifties, and they were talking and looking around for cars and crossing the street. About halfway across the man reaches over to arrange the woman's collar, and the woman reaches up to help him and without even looking at each other, all in a motion, they got the collar straightened, their hands together, and across the street."

"That's nice," I say, and sit up on the couch, look at Larry, who stands, circles once and settles again, and then at Joan.

"It was." She puts down her paintbrush and rubs her fingers into a cloth. "I like to think we could age into people who deserve that."

"We will," I tell her; then I think a minute. "We are, aren't we?"

"No-o." She draws the word out as if I'm joking. Then she looks at me, throws the cloth she's holding into the air to caricature my alarm. It doesn't make me feel better. "OK, not yet," she says.

"What are you trying to say?"

"Tucker," she says. She's smiling at me.

"You're talking about me."

"Us," she says. "No—them. I was talking about them."

You're not, I think, and then I say it, "You're not."

She doesn't say anything.

"I'm insulted," I tell her. "You should say what you mean."

She picks up the cloth and then throws it down again. She shakes her head at it lying there on the floor.

"Oh Lord, Tucker," she says. "You know what I mean. You would have had her arm twined around yours three times. You would have put her hand in your pocket or something. You—" she pauses, considers me. "You're passionate." She looks away as she's saying the word.

"And that's bad?" I'm asking her.

"No." She's drawing that word out again. "It's just—" She holds her hand in the air and puts on this patient look, as if she's going to explain something. "Passion for somebody who's not yourself isn't very, I don't know, useful." She drops her hands in her lap.

"Useful," I say. "Useful."

"Well, something like that. I don't know. I was making conversation. I was talking about a goal."

"You're saying if I were that man, we'd be what, dead in the street, run down mid swoon by a bus? Is that what you're saying?"

"I'm not saying. What I am saying is we'll have to wait and see."

She has picked up her brush again. She is preparing to ignore me.

Wait and see, I think. I look back at the TV. A woman actor is crying, telling her husband she's tired of being brave, that it's very hard to be brave. She is wasting real tears on this. I recognize her from an old sitcom they rerun after the late news, and I think of her in it, ridiculous in her outdated clothes and hairdo, sitting in a room full of ridiculous furniture that people took seriously for three months ten years ago. I resent her. There should be an immediate way to communicate to her the puny irony of her life.

"This stinks," I say out loud. Joan doesn't look up. She's poised behind her painting, as if it's important. I've never understood what she sees in them. She isn't good, and I'm not sure she even wants to be, though she paints three, four times a week, mostly still life—fruit, old wine bottles, once a pair of my shoes. She has an odd vision of things. Her apples are unabashedly red and perfectly round, her bananas completely unbruised and painted a screaming canary yellow. The black and white she saw in my old basketball shoes has a stern urgency, that sharp imperative of graphics. We hang most of her work in the kitchen, and mornings, after she leaves for the bank and I sit alone in there looking at cold coffee and the crusts of toast and my own legs, mottled and pasty in the harsh morning light, I feel surrounded, singular, unwashed, as if I've wandered by accident onto a different, perfect planet.

I look at her now, leaning over a side table, out of the beam of light and in shadow, mixing something seriously. Larry has moved to her feet, and she sits up into the light without displacing him. Then she stares at the canvas, holding her brush. She sits that way, unmoved, for a minute.

"Now I suppose you're waiting for the muse," I say. "Patiently, of course, dispassionately," I continue.

She looks at me without moving, only a flicker of her eyes, the brush still poised in her hand.

"You're snide," she says, "which is boring me." Then she pushes Larry off her feet, puts her brush down and says, "I want tea, do you?"

I say yes under my breath, wanting her to hear only my anger, and slide down on the couch, listening to the clank of the teapot and the whoosh of water. Larry brings his sock over to me, and I throw it across the room a couple times, trying to land it high enough up on Joan's chairback that he'll have to leap to get it, but he just sits and whines when the sock lands out of his reach.

"Larry," I say, going over to Joan's chair. "You are not a re-sourceful animal."

I give him one end of the sock, and he tugs at it while I look at Joan's new painting. Usually she doesn't like me to see them until she's finished and usually I respect that, but in the kitchen, her back is to me, and I sit down in her chair.

It's good. She isn't painting anything I can put my finger on— just color and line—but it's good. Streams of reds, blues, and yellows billow across the canvas like a striped flag. At their edges, the stripes overlap and settle into subtler blends, but the eye is always directed back to the center of each swath, where the color is strongest, boldest. There is something celebratory about it, something high-pitched and happy that merits the extravagance so out of place in her other paintings. I wonder why she didn't tell me she was going to try something new. I wonder what made her think of it. I feel a mixture of pride and exclusion.

Larry nudges my elbow, the sock in his mouth, and I say, "Larry, this is not you." I would have bet that Joan's next painting would be a portrait of Larry, but this thing has nothing to do with Larry or me or anything I can decipher. I want her to come in and explain it to me, but she's angry, she won't. I look at it again, and face to face with it, I think of slipping it outside the front door. Instead, I touch it lightly in the top left corner with my finger. The paint is thick and tacky, not yet dry, and I push a little harder, until I see a smudge. Then, pressing deeply with two fingers, I spell my name, my full name, John Howard Tucker, across the canvas.

I'm not sorry for the first few moments. I'm not even sure what I've done. I look at my name. Then I wipe my fingers on the cloth next to the chair and carry Larry back to the couch. I lie down on my side, pull Larry up so he can put his nose in the crook of my elbow, and look back at the TV.

Joan comes in, sets my tea on the floor, and scoots in next to Larry. She brushes her hand across my forehead and then runs it over Larry's muzzle.

"So fellas," she says. "What's on now?"

"Oh," I say.

I am so full of regret and fear that I have trouble breathing lying down. I sit up and pull Larry onto my lap. Joan moves in closer; the couch feels suddenly very crowded. She looks from me to the television and back again.

"Anything good?" she asks.

"I wrote my name," I say, losing my breath in the middle of the sentence and having to swallow, "on your painting."

"What?"

She'd heard only my stutter, and her face is kind, full of inquiry. I point to her easel.

"I wrote my name," I say, this time too loud, but her face is still frozen, kind, patient. She even has a half-smile on her face, and perhaps that is why I lean forward and speak even louder, as if to someone partially deaf or dull. "I ruined it," I say.

She stands up, still looking at me, and backs over to the easel; her face has more question than kindness in it now. Pushing my shoulders against the couch, I hold Larry and wait. I think of looking back at the television, hoping crazily, mightily, that if I look relaxed the moment will ease somehow, but the voices coming out of it sound tinny and false in the quiet room, so I watch her.

She doesn't look at it for a moment, but when she does, her shoulders fall, her arms go limp and her face loses all expression. Although she is still standing, it's as if the second she saw that canvas every muscle, tendon, cartilage—the very string and gristle of her—snapped. I watch her and think, oddly, of my father, of his corpse, and how it did not look like the man who had lived in it, but abandoned—by life or his character or soul, by every familiar and singular tension; it was only flesh and bone. I've killed her, I think. I want to throw my shoe, to startle her back.

Instead, I say her name, softly, whispering.

"Joan, Joan," I say, as though calling her in the dark.

Her head whips from the canvas to me, and then she throws everything she can get her hands on: tubes of paint, brushes, jars, an ashtray full of butts that fly into the air like confetti, even the painting itself; the corner strikes the small of my back like an arrow as I roll off the couch and sends up a low, confusing grunt of pain from deep inside my chest.

"You hurt me," I yell. "You'll hurt Larry."

But Larry has run into the kitchen, his tail between his legs, ears pressed close to his head.

"Damn you," she says, and she keeps saying it, her voice changing: loud, then fading and breathy with the effort of hurling books, her palette, her teacup. "Damn you to hell."

I stand and move toward her, my arms up around my head.

"Just stop a minute," I say. "One minute."

She puts her hand on a table lamp, a heavy, brass-bottomed lamp. "Don't touch me. Move away now," she says, backing up, trying to build a distance between us, while I move forward, closing it up. She pulls her chair in front of her, and I push it aside. When her shoulders are against the wall, she calls out, "Larry, come boy," as if he's the only thing left to stack in front of her.

"Larry, no," I shout. "Stay."

She looks straight at me then, her eyes wide in a way I don't want or deserve, and I think it's the fear I see in her face, the actual, horrified fear of me, her husband, radiating through her like a tremble, that makes me pull back my hand and hit her. I'm not sure why, somewhere between my shoulder and her face, the hand that has been flattened to slap her curls itself into a fist.

I hit her too hard. I have never hit a woman before—only men, boys. A strange thought goes through my head. That's not how you hit a woman, I think. The first thing I say is, "Oh God,

I hit you too hard," as she lies on the floor with a thin string of blood running out of her nose. The house is quiet and I am afraid to move. The sound of the television, eerily chatty behind me, makes me feel like I've walked into a house full of dead people. Larry comes in from the kitchen, his nails clicking over the linoleum, then hushed by the carpet, and walks over to Joan. He sniffs at her face, puts his nose near her closed eye. I grab him and hold him against my chest.

Joan stirs then, puts her arms out, up to her head, and moans. I hold Larry tighter and back away from her in small half steps, saying over and over, "I'm sorry. I'm sorry. I'm sorry." She opens her eyes and stares, accusing, angry, violated, at the ceiling.

Then she says, still looking at the ceiling, "It's OK. You didn't mean it." She is using a voice I don't recognize—weighty, labored, dead-sounding. "Just help me up. Put me in bed now."

I set Larry down and help her up gently, aware of limbs and effort, afraid we might become entangled, frightened of her and myself. Larry stands back, and I lead her into the bedroom, my hand cupped under one of her elbows, the way you lead an old woman across the street or up steps. I keep my hand under her elbow while she slips off her jeans. I'm listening to the odd, final sound as they slide down her legs and quietly thump on the floor—the sound of a child coming down a slide and flying into a pile of sand. I feel alert and criminal. The substance and detail of the room impress me: the nightstand littered with magazines, the second bureau drawer wedged slightly open, the closet doorknob hung with belts, but more than anything, her elbow, the way it fits into my hand like a ball into a socket. I have an awful, sacred feeling of recognition, that precise clarity of destiny thieves and priests must know, that this one moment is what all my life will be about. When I let go of her so she can take off her blouse, though, I lose hold on everything. I watch her fumble, naked, through a drawer, halting and hesitating with each small motion as though she might cry or collapse. Although I feel absent, invisible, she moves as if I have a gun trained on her.

Pulling the covers back, she crawls into bed. I tuck them up around her neck and put Larry in with her.

"Here's Larry," I say. "Larry's here. Do you want a washcloth for your nose?"

She touches the back of her hand to her lip and then looks at it.

"No," she says.

The next day is Sunday and I get up early to clean the mess, to turn the ruined painting to the wall. Then I rush out to get the paper, fresh melons, sausages, and muffins. Larry whines at the door, begging to come along, but I put him back in bed with Joan. I think she is awake and pretending not to be. All through breakfast she is quiet, precise, perfunctory, but when she kisses me for the melons, it isn't the weight of her mouth, dull and grave against mine, that bothers me so much as the crescent-shaped bruise on her right cheekbone. I can see as she raises her chin and offers the right side of her face to me that she is displaying it, that she has already examined it in the bathroom mirror and she means to present it to me in just that way, not as accusation but as fact.

Softly, I say I will do the dishes, and she watches me gather the plates and fill the sink. Then she walks over and stares out the back-door window.

"Look, I'll put Larry out and work all day," she says. "I'll just paint it again and that'll be the end of it."

Her voice surprises me. I turn off the water and look at her, but she doesn't face me. Her hands shake a little, and I watch her bury them in the pockets of her jeans. I know it is too soon to touch her, too soon to do anything, so I say, "OK. Thank you, Joan. Really."

She turns, smiles a brief smile, and says, "Come on, Larry boy. You're going out."

I read every word of the paper, thinking I should stay in the kitchen, knowing she should be alone; that, and I'm afraid to be in the same room with her and the painting. The kitchen has the feel of a hospital waiting room—still, fragile, anticipatory—but I force myself to read on. I am up to Thursday of the TV listings when I hear her shout Larry's name, and then the slam of the screen door.

I don't see anything happen. By the time I reach the front porch Joan and Larry lie stretched out against the far curb. In the middle of the street, an old station wagon with wooden side panels has stopped, and a short man with a crewcut is getting out. I'd heard his tires screech from the living room, but I'd heard no impact. For one second, I wait, watching Joan. She lies still, but I can see she's squeezing Larry, talking to him. Then she lets him go. He scampers off in two tall leaps, and Joan lies still again, her arms pressed to the pavement. I run to her then in a barefoot, clumsy way.

"What happened?" I say to the man with the crewcut. "Did you hit her? Are you all right, Joan? Don't move."

"She ran into the street," the man tells me, gesturing toward her.

"I fell down," Joan says, sitting up.

"Don't move," I tell her, and then I look at the man. "You were speeding, weren't you? The speed limit is fifteen on this street."

"I didn't touch her." He points to his car. "I stopped way back there. She was after the dog. She tripped."

I stare at him, my hands on my hips.

"I swear." He raises both hands. "Ask her."

"Oh God," Joan says. "Oh no."

Her mouth open, her face pale and slack, she's standing now, holding her arms out, as though she wants one of us to come and take them from her. From wrist to elbow, they've been scraped raw. She swings them from the driver to me, then sits down heavily on the curb, rests her forehead on her knees, and begins to rock slowly back and forth.

"Lord," the driver says.

I turn to him, and that's when I see, over his shoulder, neighbors all down the block—some still frozen on their porches, others taking the first hesitant steps across their lawns, and a whole group, housedresses, Bermuda shorts, a few kids, in determined middle-of-the-street full stride. I turn to Joan, and as I kneel beside her, I hear a woman's voice, feel it on my neck, saying, "You poor thing. We called an ambulance and it'll be just one minute."

Joan doesn't look up, just keeps rocking. I grind my knees into the street, balance one of her hands, palm up, in mine.

"It'll only be a minute," I say, touching her shoulder lightly. "Joan?"

I think I hear her say, "Don't," softly, more to the pavement than to me. "Don't." The word seems to gag her.

"Have her hold her arms up," a man's voice says. The next one I recognize—the driver of the station wagon. "Everybody should just move back and let her be."

I bend closer to Joan, wanting to have been the one to have said that, and wonder if she'll let me carry her into the house.

"Hey," I whisper. "Hey, are you all right?"

She lifts her head then, and I'm startled by her calm. Although blotchy, the bruise on her cheekbone ruddy from tears or pain, her face says not one thing has happened to her. She stares at me.

"I hate you," she says, shrugging my hand off her shoulder. "Get your hands off me."

She stands up then, and I stand with her, my hands swaying in the air on either side of her. I feel the crowd sway with me, as if suddenly Joan is two stories up, threatening to jump, and we're going to catch her.

"Wait," I tell her. "Sit still a minute."

"Get—" She stops as her eyes move to the people behind me, but they leave her unchanged. She could have been back at the breakfast table, pretending to pick at her melon, or dangling both legs from the top rail of a fire escape. She is certain.

"Away from me," she says, and pushes me once in the chest, hard. Then her voice cracks, but she goes on, pushes me in the chest again, and then again. "Stop looking at me. Stop doing things to me. Stop talking. Just stop, do you hear?"

I turn to the half-circle of neighbors, their curiosity knocked into something stolid, looking almost sleepy now, and I want to wave them all home to their living rooms, their kitchens, to coffee, to some intimacy that could never be acted out on a curb, when I see Larry sitting, ears erect, at the edge of our yard.

I point to him and look back at Joan.

"There's Larry," I say. "You got him in time."

"Both of you." She's shouting now, bent forward at the waist. "I hate you both."

Then everything does stop. The half-circle of neighbors widens, and we all just lean back to wait. Joan turns and begins to walk up the block, away from us all. She tries to wipe her face with the back of one arm and gets blood in her hair. The driver of the station wagon walks up behind her, puts his hands on her shoulders, and sits her gently back on the curb. He whispers something to her, and then he pats at the blood in her hair with his handkerchief. She trembles when he does it, but she lets him.

"Why don't you all move off a little?" he calls to us. "You're upsetting her." I stare at his handkerchief.

"She's my wife," I say. "She might be in shock or something. I'm her husband."

"I'm not." She looks at the driver and then at the neighbors when she says it, and they move forward. Joan turns away then, and starts to cry hard and silently. Her arms shake in front of her, and she folds them stiffly into her lap. Two women still dressed for church come and sit beside her on the curb. The rest of the crowd closes around them.

Next to me in the street is the end of Larry's rope. I pick it up. It's wet where he chewed through it. Winding it around my hand I follow it to the edge of our lawn where Larry still sits, and I watch a little girl run up the walk and into our house, letting the screen door slide shut behind her. A second later she comes out again, taking the last step of the porch with a small skip, Joan's purse swinging from her shoulder.

"The lady told me to," she says when she sees me.

Scooping Larry up I see the blood on my shirt where Joan pushed me and on his fur where she squeezed him. I press him to my chest. A nearing siren is the only sound. It draws Larry's ears up, and he begins to tremble.

"I'm taking my dog in the house," I say, but no one looks up. "He's upset, and I'll be right back."

But I don't go right back. I stand at the front window holding Larry, half-hidden by the drape, and watch an ambulance pull up and two men in blue coats who wear their pants belted under their bellies like cowboys wrap Joan's arms in gauze and then help her into the back of the van gently, cautiously, a hand under each elbow, the way I'd helped her into bed the night before.

Mothers
without
Children

———————

Joy brings the meeting to order. A huge pious woman who does not diet, she maintains she is happy the way she is. Two hundred and thirty-six pounds, she says flatly, not prideful, not rueful either. Next to her, Charlene, a wraith with a frightened reedy voice many of us in the group find unnerving, as if someone or something has squeezed her windpipe partially shut, looks vaguely ashamed. It's difficult to know if she's ashamed because Joy weighs 236 pounds or because Joy is comfortable speaking facts.

Joy leads our prayer. She says, "Father, watch over our children. Forgive the men. Hold us from hatred. Help us to know they've stolen our children, not our souls."

We all say Amen, except Annalise. At Annalise's first meeting we noted her silence, and Joy explained to her that we did not mean the opening prayer to offend, that of course different people had different ideas of God. For some, he was the force of creation; for others, a force inside themselves; for others, a force inside the group. All that was fine with us, Joy said.

Annalise looked unaffected, which drew our curiosity. At our first meetings most of us had been shy or tearful or explosive, but Annalise maintained a brittle poise. She smoked premium-length cigarettes, one after the other, drawing them delicately from a hard leather case she wore clipped to the belt of her blue jeans.

"I believe in God," Annalise told Joy that night. "The same one you do. The one who sees all and hears all and does all. And I want him to know I'm angry, that he screwed up, that yes, yes, all of eternity without a mistake, but here it is. Me. This. You."

Tonight, as we wait for someone to begin, Annalise stares across the circle at Barbara, who shared with us last week that she had taken a lover, her first, who is a woman, also her first. She worried about what she called "the drama" of such a choice. Hadn't there been enough drama in her life, she said, as if there were a limit on how much drama one life could contain. Tonight, under Annalise's attention, Barbara fidgets, moving her long feet, which she had tucked under her in the chair, back to the floor.

"You know, I've been mulling you over," Annalise says to her. "You and your new girlfriend. And I think you're soft-pedaling the issue. I want men to know that I reject them categorically. If I could, I'd wear a sign. And I want them to know it's not a matter of some erotic preference. It's just good judgment. They're killers."

Annalise has two boys, six and eight, missing for just over a year. Twice, on their birthdays, her husband has mailed her locks of their hair. About her own sons Annalise once said, "When I find them, I'll beat them bloody. I'll cook them for dinner. I'll devour them."

Tonight Joy smiles at her and says, "Anger is empowerment, too."

Irene, a tremulous woman, dainty and prim, with tiny hands and feet, nods first at Annalise, then at Barbara, then at Joy. Immediately the rest of us look at the floor. Irene was on a talk show last week, though we warned her against it. She was just a member of the audience, but they paid her plane fare out there to tell her story from the front row. Some of us got together to watch. When Irene's turn came to speak, she stood, swallowed, and nodded at the camera twice. Two thousand miles away, we sat frozen in our chairs as her eyes filled up. She just stood there.

Come on, Irene, we thought.

The host put his hand on her shoulder and lowered his eyes.

"My daughter," Irene said, quivering under his hand. She looked wildly around the studio and said it again. "My daughter." No more words came.

The host sat her down gently, looked at his feet a little longer, and went on.

Oh no, we thought. Irene.

It's her first meeting back, but so far no one has mentioned the show, our eyes flitting around the room, avoiding the subject in each other's faces. In the vicinity of Annalise, though, Irene stands suddenly and breaks for the door, her face puffy with emotion. Near the cookies and coffeepot she turns back to us, throws her patent-leather pocketbook to the floor, and then slides down the wall, weeping.

"I couldn't even tell the story." She speaks between sobs. "My God, what if she saw me? What if she saw me like that?"

Joy picks up the pocketbook, tucks it under Irene's arm, and leads her out to the car. No one says anything. Annalise takes longer than is necessary to crush out her cigarette. This is self-help, Joy has told us before, but sometimes you have to lean.

A new girl, young, probably not yet thirty, but with strands of gray scattered through her long dark hair, begins to cry. She is pregnant, and we find this notable, yet unmentionable. Raising her face from her handkerchief she tells us that her new husband feels she should try now to quiet her interest in the missing child. He has encouraged her to buy new curtains and bedding and baby clothes.

"It isn't that he says so," she tells us, "but in his silences, even in his body as he makes love to me, I think he believes he should be powerful enough to obliterate what happened. 'It won't ever happen again,' is what he says."

She buries her face in her handkerchief again, and we watch her shoulders heave. Then she raises her chin, looks solemnly at us. It hurts to look back at her. "He doesn't change *any*thing," is what she says.

We look to each other, to the door, but Joy doesn't appear. Even Annalise is restive, struggling to open a new pack of cigarettes.

"You have to believe your child is alive and safe," Charlene says. "She's just somewhere else, sleeping and getting up in the morning and maybe going to school."

Annalise expels a stream of smoke. "How can you be so mild, Charlene. Get out of your chair, at least, if you mean to help someone. Are you afraid you'll muss your hair?" She turns to the new girl. "Listen, you look young enough to hunt him down, pull a trigger, and still survive the prison term."

We sit quietly then. It's possible that Joy drove Irene home. Perhaps that's why we think of Joy's story, and why we tell it to the new one, as if it were our story or her story and in it were form, the bare scaffolding of meaning, the answer she's asking for.

After Joy's husband took her three boys and all their money she sold what he'd left behind, bought a van, and went after him. For twenty-two months she lived on the road, never even checking into a motel. She slept at highway rest stops, woke, sat up, and drove. She knew she'd find them. For fifteen years she'd lived with that man, and she knew the limits of his imagination. He was a man who considered standard vacation spots obscure. In fifteen years they'd taken fifteen vacations. To the Grand Canyon, Mt. Rushmore, the Smoky Mountains. How hard could it be? Each day opened like a promise.

She found them in Galveston, looked through the screen door of a cabin he'd rented and saw her two youngest, then four and six, eating cereal from bowls on the living room floor. They stood up and pressed their spines against the wall when they saw her, and they wouldn't come near, not even when she whispered their names. Outside, the oldest one, Frank, who was twelve, must have watched her drive up because she turned to see him, breathless and possessed, taking a baseball bat to her van. She ran to him, and the younger ones followed, the baby crying, tugging at his brother's clothes as he smashed Joy's headlights, her windshield, her side mirrors.

"What are we doing, Frankie," the youngest screeched. "What are we doing?"

Suddenly Joy's husband was behind them at the screen door shouting, "Franklin Marshall Howard, you stop that."

Frank did, staring wildly at his father and then throwing the bat as far as he could. It clattered across the street and wedged in the mouth of a storm drain. Joy took a step toward him, and though his face was dirty and streaked with tears, she saw the new shadow of a mustache just above his lip. It brought her hand to her own mouth. He ran furiously away from her, cutting behind houses, the two little ones following, pleading after him, "Frankie, Frankie."

Joy's husband stood still in the doorway, but she walked right past him to the van, scooped glass out of her seat, got in, and went after her boys, driving circles through the neighborhood, calling their names through the broken windshield, screaming details of their pasts: Frankie, you had a blue trike when you were three, with a bell you loved to ring. And Jerry, you ate strawberries every summer from the garden. And in the winter you all three went sledding on Carter's Hill. And Tommy, you were afraid—my baby, my littlest boy—of the mailman and spiders and bees. You *know* me, she called out to them. I know *you*.

Men stopped in yards as she passed, held rakes. She took a wrong turn and was driving erratically, frantic for a street she recognized, when the police pulled her over. One officer helped her find the house again, but they were already gone, the clothes dryer still running on a back porch off the kitchen.

The story silences the new girl—and us, too. We sit in our chairs, a curl of smoke rising from Annalise's cigarette. None of us has ever gotten that close: To see our child's face, its features shifted ever so slightly from the arrangement in old snapshots we carry. To watch our child *eat*. To see our child's chest rise and fall in a tremble of breath under a thin tee-shirt. For that moment we would forget all the breath that has moved and continues to move them into a future without us. Like Joy, we would call out the details we carry, open our kit bags to remind them of toys and pets and friends and rooms and days they've forgotten. We'd insist they knew us. And *Sweetie, Scoopalopodus, Ballerinatina*, we'd say, *I know you.* Finally, then, our personal tragedies would fall away. We would be like any parent, every parent, all our children gone, looking for the dead, believing that when we find them they will stare blankly at us, and then, hearing the call of our stories, blink back to life.

Roll

Louise woke late—at least she thought it was late from the band of sunlight glowing yellow around the edge of her bedroom window shade—and so she washed and dressed and combed her hair quickly, then tiptoed to the sofa bed in the living room where Charlotte and Albert slept.

"We have to meet Nana Marge for Mass." Louise had meant to speak quietly, but Charlotte opened her eyes as if she'd been struck, then stared at the ceiling.

"Please," Charlotte said.

"He's asleep." Louise whispered now. "He won't know if he's asleep."

Charlotte raised her head to look at Albert, who slept in his white tee-shirt like a boy, one arm thrown over his eyes, the sheet pulled up to his chin. Then she lay her head back on her pillow and fumbled on the floor next to the bed for her house slipper.

"I'm going to throw this at the spot you're standing in, Louise," she said when she found it. "If you're standing there when it lands, you get hit. It's nobody's fault but yours."

As Louise turned the corner onto Armour Boulevard she saw Nana Marge waiting half a block down in front of her hotel, adjusting the set of her hat in the tinted front window and checking the pockets of her powder blue duster as if she'd forgotten something. Even from that distance, Louise could see Nana Marge was angry, so she slowed down, pretending to be interested in the sale bins of rubber beach thongs and blow-up water toys someone had stacked along the wall of the Parkview Drug.

"Oh please, child," she heard Nana Marge call out. "Like any of that would last as long as a carton of milk."

When Louise reached her Nana Marge said, "She's home in bed with whosis, isn't she?"

"I don't think she feels well this morning," Louise said.

"Oh, she feels just fine. She feels better than either one of us, standing out here on the hot pavement in our Sunday best. She feels better than the two of us put together will probably feel all day. Look behind you, child." Nana Marge put her hands on Louise's shoulders and turned her around. "What does that clock over the Parkview say?"

Louise squinted to see it through the wavy glare of heat. The little hand was on the ten. She opened her mouth to say so.

"It says Mass was over twenty minutes ago." Nana Marge gave her a small shove. "It says if someone doesn't pay you some mind you're going to grow up to be a rock."

Louise closed her mouth.

"Today is August 15," Nana Marge went on, "the Feast of Our Lady's Assumption, which means we've missed a holy day of obligation, by the way, and which also means school starts in exactly two weeks. I'll bet every stitch of clothing I have on that she hasn't been down to enroll you yet."

She turned Louise around again and looked her dead in the eye. "You miss another year of school, and you'll end up just like her. And what is she good at? The woman could take a job drowning kittens."

"I think she's going to sign me up tomorrow," Louise said.

"Tomorrow," Nana Marge turned back to her hotel. "Tomorrow means day old bread."

At the revolving door she stopped and patted her pockets again. Louise wondered if she was thinking of Theo, a crooked, trembling Chihuahua Nana Marge had carried everywhere after arthritis ruined his matchstick legs. A retired seamstress who lived at the hotel had sewn special pockets into all of Nana Marge's clothes for him, and after he died, Nana Marge bought a ceramic statue of a Chihuahua, almost as big as Theo had been, which she kept on a side table next to the daybed where Louise slept last summer after Charlotte disappeared with her last boyfriend, Roy. Sometimes at night a piece of moonlight sneaked through the slice in Nana Marge's drapes to fall on the statue, and Louise had to turn its odd glassy stare to the wall before she could fall asleep.

"I need to sit down before I fall down," Nana Marge said. "Before I die on a holy day in a state of sin."

They sat on the bus bench at the corner, where the sun had warmed the slats beneath them, and above them the sky, streaked with yellow and pink, looked like soft taffy. Louise felt almost glad they had missed church, which was stifling on summer days. One morning last year, not long after Charlotte disappeared, Louise fainted coming down the wide aisle after Mass, a muffling darkness closing around her in the slow crowd, blotting out the soft voices above her and the backs of women's pastel dresses, shrinking the whole huge world of the cathedral down to a pinpoint of light, then swallowing that, too. Someone soaked a cloth diaper in the drinking fountain and threw it over her face to revive her, and that's how Louise woke, opening her eyes into a white fog, the damp cloth filling her mouth when she breathed in to scream.

Sitting next to Louise on the bench, Nana Marge set her purse upright, then flat in her lap, then reached up again to adjust her hat, a small circle of blue and white cloth flowers with pearl centers, held on her head by two plastic combs, one of which, Louise could see through Nana Marge's thin hair, had left a painful scarlet bite in the soft scalp behind her ear.

"Is your hat too tight?" Louise asked.

Nana Marge touched the tender spot behind her ear.

"It is," she said. "It fits me like a cheap shoe."

She seemed tired after she said that. She closed her eyes briefly, then opened them again, turning to Louise.

"I'm guessing they were out all night."

"No, ma'am," Louise said, though they had been. For the last couple weeks Charlotte and Albert had been driving to a new place miles up the river, almost to St. Joseph, a dance hall where the ceiling was covered with silver foil leaves that rustled whenever the dancers moved.

"It sounds like people whispering," Charlotte had told her the night before, and then turned to lean hard against the stove, raising her chin so that her long neck showed white, while behind her the franks and beans she was warming for Louise's dinner bubbled too hard.

"Whispering underwater," she said then. "Something impossible like that."

From her chair at the kitchen table Louise saw that the circle of flame under the pot was dangerously close to a soft fold in Charlotte's dancing dress, and though the fire never touched the material, Louise watched as a small brown-edged tear opened in the filmy fabric just above Charlotte's waist. She saw Charlotte's skin.

"Charlotte," Louise said, but in the same moment Albert tapped at the screen door, and Charlotte moved away from the stove to let him in, resting her hands palm up on the square shoulders of his suit as if he'd caught her still damp from preparing some fancy meal.

"Eat your beans," Albert said over Charlotte's shoulder when he saw Louise watching. "Mind your Ps and Qs."

Louise hadn't known fire could do that, burn what it hadn't even touched, and after they were gone, she sat alone at the kitchen table in the darkening apartment, jumping at every stray noise, afraid of something she couldn't name.

Nana Marge reached over to lift Louise's hair off her shoulders. "It's too hot for all this hair," she said, "and you're too thin to carry it around."

"Charlotte wants to keep it long now. She says it makes me look light and easy."

"Light and easy," Nana Marge said. "You've got a rat tangle in there as old as you are."

Louise leaned forward, away from her hand, and Nana Marge stood slowly.

"Go ahead," she said. "I'm all out of ideas. You go on home and wake her up and make her cook something."

At home, the apartment was quiet, the shades still drawn in the living room, and Louise hesitated outside the front door, standing on tiptoe to peek into the hallway, where she saw Charlotte's house slipper. Probably they were still asleep, and so Louise lowered herself to her heels and went around back to sit on the stoop until they were up.

Bic, Mrs. Belwicker's boy from the next door apartment, was already home from church and out in the yard digging a hole. He looked up as she stepped through the day lilies at the side of their building.

"I got a new shovel." He held up a battered shovel with a dull and dented edge for her to see.

"Oh." Louise nodded.

"Found it." He pointed down the slope of their backyard to the scattering of tin outbuildings behind the bus barn on the next block. "Down by the old streetcar tracks."

"Oh," she said again and then, when she saw that he was still watching her, added, "What are you digging for?"

"Last spring I buried a dead baby squirrel. My dad bet me I won't be able to find it." He squinted at the hole. "He says even bones disappear after enough time."

As he drove the old shovel into the loose sandy soil of the yard the muscles in his back stretched and then rolled when he came up with a heavy load, which he shook out carefully over a pile next to the hole. Although he was only a year older than Louise, with his chest bare and streaks of sweat running down the dust on his face he looked like a small-sized man. If the bones were there, Louise thought, he would probably find them.

"Hey," she called. "Bic."

"What?"

"What happens in school?"

He stopped in a crouch, looking over his shoulder at her, then stood up straight. "My mom says she's going to tell if you don't go this year. She told my dad she's going to call someone, even though my dad said not to."

"I'm going," Louise said. "I'm going in two weeks. Tell me what happens."

"I don't know." He rested one foot on his shovel. "We go to Mass every day at Perpetual Help." Looking past her at the house, he said, "Is your mom in there?"

"Yes."

"I heard yelling this morning," he said. "And crying."

Louise stood up and looked behind her at the back door where the kitchen shade was pulled tight. She thought of the house slipper and sat down again. "She's in there with Albert. Last night he took her someplace up the river. A dance hall with leaves on the ceiling," she said.

Bic nodded distantly, still looking past her. "They don't even make that car he drives anymore, you know. My dad said he had a red one like it when he was a teenager that he called the red sled."

Louise knew what he meant was that he had never seen the like. Bic's mother had huge hips, fastened her hair back and cooked a hot lunch every day, even when she was home alone with Bic's baby sister. Every afternoon she sat down at the small kitchen table just inside the back door with a plate of stew or a slice of meat loaf or a warmed-up bowl of navy bean soup. Louise had seen her through the screen.

"Just tell me what you do when you first go into school, okay? The very first thing you do."

"What?" Bic said. "In the morning?"

"Yeah."

"Well, the bell rings and you sit down and the first thing they do is take roll."

"Roll," Louise said.

"Attendance. Sister Anthony likes to say your whole name—first, baptismal, and last. She might have just finished calling me Bic at the door, but then she picks up her green book and calls out, Richard Joseph Belwicker. After she says your name, you say, 'Here.' That's about it. She marks it in her book."

"Then what?"

"Then school starts. Once they know you're there, they tell you what to do."

Louise nodded. At Mass she'd seen the young nun who directed the youth choir putting the children in line, aiming them silently, with only a light touch on the shoulder, into place.

Just then, from somewhere in the house, Charlotte shouted, "Leave it alone, will you? Leave it. Just leave it alone." A door slammed, and then it was quiet again. Suddenly Mrs. Belwicker was out the back door of her place and on the porch next to Louise, her baby, Teresa, balanced on one hip.

"Bic," she called. "Go get some milk at Sam's."

"Forget it," Bic drove his shovel into the ground.

"Whole milk," she said. "For your sister."

He let go of the shovel and slumped by his mother who pulled some soft bills from her apron and tucked them into his back pocket. "Put on a shirt," she told him.

After he'd gone inside Mrs. Belwicker stood a moment next to Louise, but Louise stared out at Bic's shovel, which stood upright in the yard, and then at the hole, already deeper than Bic would have dug to bury a baby squirrel. She wondered how the ground did that, if the bones had really disappeared or only drifted apart and down so deep they'd never be found.

"Do you want to hold baby Teresa?" Mrs. Belwicker asked.

"No, ma'am," Louise said. Then she added, "Thank you, though."

"If anything happens, you come tap at my back door."

"I will," Louise said. The soft boards of the stoop gave under her as Mrs. Belwicker took a few slow steps away. Louise heard the screen door squeak open, then stop.

"Well," Mrs. Belwicker said, "you better get in there."

Louise stood up slowly and walked around the side of the building, where, outside the front door, she sat awhile longer in the sun. Then she went in, picking up Charlotte's house slipper and carrying it with her into her room. Lying back on her bed, she pressed her cheek against her pillow and smelled the common, earthy odor of her sleep. When Charlotte passed her door wearing only a slip, Louise sat up.

"Leave your dress on," Charlotte said. "Albert's going to take us to Eagles."

Rubbing her hand over the braided ribbon on Charlotte's house slipper, Louise sat still, and Charlotte stepped just inside the room to lean against the doorway, looking thin and cool in her slip.

"What?" Charlotte asked.

Louise put the slipper on the floor next to the bed. "Mrs. Belwicker says you're going to run off and leave me again."

Crossing her arms, Charlotte tipped her head back, looked at the ceiling. "Mrs. Belwicker is fat and tired. Mrs. Belwicker thinks God made trees to keep the sun off her head."

"Are you?"

She lowered her chin until she looked Louise in the eye. "No."

Charlotte had a full, pretty mouth, pink even when she didn't paint it and always parted slightly like a child in sleep. She could have been lying.

"Damn Louise, he's got a brother-in-law in San Antonio who could put him to work tomorrow. I've got to check out opportunities, that's all. I'm not going to run off and leave you." She eased onto the edge of the bed next to Louise, sat a moment, then pulled her under one arm. "You've just been to church with Nana Marge, is all."

"Don't," Louise said, her mouth pressed against the slick material of Charlotte's slip.

Charlotte stood up and backed toward the door. "Pardon me," she said.

"I mean don't leave me here," Louise said quickly.

"I'm *not*." She reached out to give Louise's shoulders a small shake. "Now wash your face. We'll go down to Eagles and you can play some pinball."

"I don't want to go there."

"Fine. Stay here. Let moss grow up your back. Take your tea with Mrs. Belwicker."

She closed the door behind her and Louise sat still, listening to the sound of Charlotte's light footsteps and then Albert's heavier ones. When she jumped up and fled into the hallway, they stood dressed at the door, Charlotte in a pair of slacks and sleeveless sweater, Albert in the same suit he'd worn the night before, his shirt collar open now, folded flat against his square shoulders.

"I'm coming," she said.

"Put your hat on, then," Albert told her, heading out the door. "Keep the flies out of your eyes."

Because she didn't own a hat or know what he meant, Louise hesitated, but he was already walking across the yard in the light, rolling way he had, as if he were on wheels.

In Albert's car Louise sat in back on the slick tan upholstery while Charlotte rode up front, one hand balanced gently on Albert's neck, just along the white line of his haircut. Nana Marge told Charlotte once that Albert was a dandy, a man who substituted cologne for character, but Charlotte said Nana Marge had never had anything in her life that wasn't broken down or used up, so how could she know. Leaning forward, Louise rested her chin on the top of the front seat.

"Bic likes this car," she said.

"Bic, huh?" Albert said.

"That's the neighbor boy. It's his nickname."

Albert sat quietly, eyes fixed on the road.

"Short for Richard," Louise said.

"Richard." Albert raised his chin and his eyebrows when he said it, pronouncing the word snootily, through pursed lips. When Charlotte laughed he put one hand on her knee. "Richard my ass," he said.

At Eagles, which was a narrow bar and grill run by a man named Tony who had gone to school with Charlotte, Albert gave Louise four quarters for pinball, and she slid them all into the baseball machine. On the bonus ball of her first game a man came and stood behind her, but she was doing so well that she didn't feel shy about him watching. She'd never earned a bonus ball before. Just as she landed it in the extra innings chute, she felt the man lift her hair from her shoulders and hold it loosely in his hands. She straightened slowly, letting her own hands fall from the machine as the ball jumped out of the chute and rolled through the flippers. Without turning around she edged delicately away, arching her neck as a tangle in her hair caught, loosened, and then fell away from the man's fingers.

"Did you lose all my money already?" Albert asked when she came to stand beside their table. His legs thrown out in front of him, the arms of the chair hooked under his own arms, he'd arranged himself so that he was almost lying down. Louise didn't know what to say to him.

"I'll bet she's hungry," Charlotte said.

"Ugh." Pulling his drink closer to him, Albert poked at the ice in his glass. "Don't eat in front of me, okay?"

Separating two bills from a stack on the table, Charlotte said, "Go eat at the bar, Louise. Tell Tony to give you a hamburger and coke."

When he saw her Tony motioned Louise down to the end of the bar farthest from the door. Normally he didn't allow kids in his place, but he let Charlotte bring Louise in as a special favor.

"The cheeseburger kid," he called out, and Louise nodded, though she didn't like cheese on her hamburger and didn't know why Tony called her that. After swiping at the bar with a rag, he slid a bowl of peanuts down in front of her.

"I got a good joke for you," he said.

Louise nodded again. Jokes made her nervous, the way the comedy shows Nana Marge liked to watch on TV made her nervous. Something bad would happen to someone and then everyone would laugh. Once Nana Marge told her that the laughter on those TV shows was really just a tape of people laughing long ago at something else.

"Most of those people laughing are in their graves. That's the real joke," Nana Marge said.

Tony's joke was about a parrot, and he told it leaning away from the bar so that other people could hear. Because she was pretty sure something bad was going to happen to the parrot Louise tried not to listen, staring instead at Tony's hair, black and shiny, combed high in the middle and slicked back along the sides so that Tony looked a little like a bird himself. When he finished the joke the others at the bar laughed, and Louise looked quickly away from Tony's hair to a shot glass full of tiny plastic swords. The corners of her mouth twitched oddly, the way they did when she was about to cry.

Tony ducked to catch her eye. "So funny you forgot to laugh, huh?"

When he saw her face he straightened, glancing briefly behind her, probably to Charlotte and Albert's table.

"That's okay," he said softly before he moved away from her. "Laughing's not required."

Louise wanted to go home. Swinging her stool around she saw Charlotte sitting with her cheek balanced on one hand, nodding at something Albert was whispering low and fast into her ear. Probably he was telling her lies, Louise thought. Charlotte's last boyfriend Roy told her he had some important job at a club in New Orleans, and that's where she'd gone with him, but he hadn't had a job at all; he just liked New Orleans. When she got back, Charlotte showed Louise on a map where it was. You just followed the Missouri river to where it emptied into the Mississippi and then followed that down to where it emptied into the sea. That's where she had been the whole time.

Across the room "Happy Birthday" started to play on the jukebox, and Louise turned to watch a table of people sing to a sleepy-looking man whose head wobbled on the end of his long neck like a hat on a stick. In front of him on the table a box sat open, and Louise raised her chin, wondering what kind of gift a man like that would get. Next to him a large woman raised herself with effort, then spread her arms wide, rolls of flesh pressing against the thin material of her blouse as she sang much too high, her voice wobbling crazily like the man's head.

When the song ended she sat down and threw her arms hard around the man's shoulders so that they both tipped one way and then the other, like a kid's roly-poly toy, until the man's head slipped through the circle of her arms and slid down her front like a sack of sugar to her lap. As the woman struggled to lift him, he began to giggle.

"I gotta go," Louise heard him say as the woman tried to set him upright. His giggle changed to a wheezing open-mouthed laugh that made it hard for him to speak. Although his mouth formed words, no sound came out.

"I got to go *now*," he finally said.

All at once his friends and the woman stood, working together to lift him from his chair, but suddenly the man appeared to be asleep, his head lolling back on his neck, arms drifting loose over the woman's round shoulders.

"Hold on, honey," she told him.

They had just gotten him to his feet and leaned against the wall when Louise saw his pants darken at the crotch. Although she wanted to look away, she didn't, afraid if she moved she might wet herself. Behind her, Tony banged the bar with the flat of both hands, and Louise jumped.

"Filth," he shouted. He threw a bar rag that caught the woman square in the back. "Get that filth out of here."

"It's his birthday," the woman screeched. She tried to cover the dark spot on the man's trousers with napkins she picked out of a dispenser, but the thin paper drifted to the floor.

"Get him out," Tony yelled. "Throw him in the goddamn street." When he saw Louise looking at him, he shouted to Charlotte to get her out, too.

"No more kids in here," he said. "No kids in this joint anymore."

In the car Charlotte and Albert were quiet. A storm had moved through while they were in Eagles, darkening the sky. Even the streetlights had come on. Charlotte rolled down her window, resting her head on the door frame so that her hair and the damp flowery smell of it floated back toward Louise. Albert lit a cigarette, then lay his arm across the back of the seat. As he turned smoothly onto the viaduct that curved around their neighborhood Louise leaned back against the cool seat, listening to the tires throw up a hissing mist. Each time a streetlight passed over them she closed her eyes, wishing they could drive for a long time. She didn't want to go home to lie quietly in her bed, the door closed and the strip of light beneath it interrupted by stray shadows.

Then the rain came again, drumming the roof of the car as Charlotte rolled her window up and slid across the seat to rest her head on Albert's shoulder. Easing off the viaduct to a stoplight they sat a moment, even after the light turned green, before Albert swung the car onto Armour. Louise sat up, suddenly alert, and looked over Charlotte's shoulder as Albert rolled the car to a stop at the curb in front of Nana Marge's hotel.

The three of them sat silently in the car while outside the rain slackened and then stopped. Charlotte didn't raise her head until Albert slipped away from her, got out, and walked around the car to open the door on the passenger side. Then she turned and pulled the seat forward.

"No," Louise said. "You promised."

Charlotte drew one arm up and lay her head in the cradle of her elbow, as if she meant to go to sleep. When she spoke, her voice was muffled.

"He really does have a job in San Antonio, Louise. That was the promise. We'll send for you and you can take the train down."

Albert stooped to speak through the open door. "It'll be a big train," he said, like that might be something she'd be sorry she missed. "With a dining car."

Louise looked past him to Nana Marge's hotel, the lobby quiet and dark except for a small lamp over the front desk. It looked later than it was inside that hotel, like a hotel full of old people who were already in bed. She pressed herself against the back seat.

"That wasn't the promise," she said to Albert. "You don't know anything."

Albert hesitated, his hands on his knees, and Louise felt him watching her. Then he came back around and got in the car, leaving her door standing open.

Charlotte raised her head then, her mouth a tight straight line. "Go on." She shook the seat once for emphasis. "Right now."

Stepping into the street, Louise's legs felt odd under her, heavy, the way they felt once when she rode a bike too far. She stood a moment beside the car.

"Get in there," Charlotte said.

Inside one slice of the hotel's revolving door Louise turned to watch them drive away. When she saw their tail lights disappear down Broadway she pushed the door around and came out again. A damp wind ruffled her clothes as she walked a few steps, then stopped. From the little bar next door to the hotel she heard low music and the murmur of voices. Someone had turned on the neon sign that said Tap Room and propped open the door so that a crooked rectangle of light glowed on the wet sidewalk. Just then a man and woman struggled out the door, and Louise stepped back against the shadow of the hotel as the woman, a pretty young stranger in a thin dress, took long steps toward the street. Stopping at the curb she turned once on her tiptoes inside the circle of the man's arms, then rested her head on the slope of his neck. When she saw Louise she smiled crookedly, her mouth a blurry red slash.

"Well," she said. "Look who's here."

Never,
Ever,
Always

My husband often traced what he called the minor flaws of my character to Kansas City, Missouri, a city he placed in the dead middle of the Midwest, a "stunningly homogenous" town, he liked to say, where it must have been horrifyingly easy for me to grow up believing untruths about the world. Often enough I agreed with him about my hometown. I grew up there the over-protected and only child of a doting, widowed mother, and I grew up there a Catholic girl. The way I remember it is as a nine-year-old in the back of Sister Mary Benedict's catechism class, as a girl tall and smart and timid enough to be trusted back there, out of Sister Mary Benedict's reach, left to my own resources.

In Sister Mary Benedict's catechism class we mainly discussed sin—sins of omission and commission, venial sins, and mortal sins. We were twenty-five girls preparing for the sacrament of penance. On Good Friday we would line up outside Father Lucardo's confessional and bare our souls for the first time. Sister Mary Benedict wanted us to feel, in those last few days, the privilege of our own redemption. She urged us to imagine a flock of white birds mired in sticky tar suddenly breaking free and clean.

Pretty girls who sat in a cluster near the coat rack tried to charm Sister Mary Benedict with claims that they had no true sins, none that mattered anyway, none that weren't eased by something as simple as the Confiteor recited at daily Mass. Someday they might commit sin, they told her—it was possible that someday they might commit even mortal sin—but when they were grown, when they were *women*. They shifted in their chairs at the word. They rolled their eyes at one another. Watching them, I saw that the idea of womanhood embarrassed them—much the same as the idea of sin embarrassed them—sin and womanhood both distant, querulous predictions. I had to raise my hand a long time before Sister Mary Benedict noticed me.

"Sister," I said, standing next to my chair. "Suppose I had committed a sin, but then I was deeply sorry in my own heart. And suppose I was *on my way* to the church to confess when a milk truck ran me down."

In a black-and-white movie my mother had watched on Saturday afternoon while she combed out my hair, I'd seen a man run down by a milk truck. He had been on his way to tell a woman that he loved her. The woman was a beautiful invalid. She loved him, too, but out of pride or misguided kindness, she had never told him. In her wheelchair she took the news of the man's death stoically while my mother's tears ran down my bare shoulders.

Sister Mary Benedict was a tall nun, heavy and hard except for her long milk-white hands. The weathered skin around her eyes pinched into furrows at my question, and the pretty girls quieted. I stood waiting next to my chair. Two white bows held my hair away from my face, which then was the blank, open face of a girl in a movie, the face of a girl who thought runaway milk trucks were about the limit of injustice in the world.

"God would still welcome me, wouldn't he, Sister?" I asked. "He'd open his arms, right?"

Sister Mary Benedict tucked her hands inside her habit and arranged them secretly at her waist. I watched her and thought oddly, "She's a woman inside those clothes—like my mother or the invalid that man died trying to reach." A flush spread under her cheekbones, and I worried for a moment that she'd known my thoughts, that she was angry. When my mother was angry she opened her pocketbook and threw things—tubes of lipstick, car keys, crumpled tissues—but Sister Mary Benedict stood still and dire as a beam of light, her eyes only on me. I saw then the answer to another question I'd once pondered alone back in the far corner of her class. That question had been: Why would she do it—give up men, cars, cologne, color, and desire? I saw then that she'd done it to become what she was at that moment—a woman in black about to pass on cruel facts to a stupid, winsome girl.

"God would not welcome you, Nora." She spoke quietly, lowering her eyes when she said my name. Then she looked at me again. "You would die alone and outside His love."

The pretty girls smirked at me as I sat down, but I thought, *Okay. All right.* I believed her. In my mind, God was a man, and though I had never really known any men outside of Father Lucardo, I had seen him often enough—sitting in Sister Mary Benedict's chair, asking each girl to stand as he read aloud in stentorian tones the grades from her quarterly report—to understand that some part of a man's stature or his calling must allow him or require him to be merciless.

That night after my bath I sat again at my mother's feet in the soft light of the TV while she put up my hair. She dipped a wooden wide-toothed comb into scented water, ran it through my hair, then wound sections up in strips of soft flannel. I leaned my cheek against her solid knee. She was watching her favorite variety show. On it, three girls in elaborate wigs sang a sad song about all the trouble they'd had after they'd gone out into the world and forgotten what their mothers told them. They'd lost their shy and happy homes. They'd lost their pasts. They'd lost their hearts, they sang. I sat up between my mother's knees. The girls blinked glamorous, affecting tears under their moun-

tains of hair. They sang words like *Never, Ever, Always*. I believed them, too.

"Gullibility is not a victimless crime," was what my husband
liked to say. He said it was no wonder I grew up to be such a
strange long-suffering woman, frightened of my own need, inor-
dinately interested in doing the right thing. My husband married
me more gently than his opinions imply. When we met he was
a tough, suspicious, hair-trigger sort of man—easily angered,
quick to push back his chair and walk away—but in my presence, he quieted, he settled, and he listened as I rambled through
a set of stories I believed must represent the central confusions of
my life. "You know, you think too much," he told me once across
a table in a crowded restaurant. "You study your life like it's an
equation, like you expect an answer." When he said it I knew he
was right, but I was not ashamed because I also knew he was a
little mesmerized by and a little protective of the frailty of my
hope. Standing to leave the restaurant that night he took my elbow gently in his hand, and I felt him feel, perhaps for the first
time, the delicacy that underlies any true authority. He looked at
me for a moment, and then he steered me out of the restaurant.

So it was lightly that my husband eased me away from home
and church, from my mother, from many of my qualities. There
were times I admired him more than I did myself. He had been,
before he met me, an adventurer. He'd gone places. He'd done
things. Once, on a bluff overlooking a cornfield where we'd
stopped to rest coming back from a day trip to the country, he
told me a story about waking up from an opium sleep to an earth-
quake in Burma. Hanging in a hammock, he'd been dreaming, he
said, of a deep rumble, the sound of a plane touching down. When
he opened his eyes he saw the treetops above him shiver eerily in
no wind, and when he sat up, the ground rose with him and then
bowed away from him, undulating in a slow wave that carried a
small shed at the edge of his clearing down a ravine. There was
no one around—the man who had rented him the hut lived half
a day's walk through the jungle—and there was no sound but the
rumble and the crack of falling trees. My husband, though, felt a

strange calm. Finally, he said, he'd gotten far enough away from all he'd been and known. There didn't seem to be anything he could or should do. He watched a huge tree fall slowly to crush a line of smaller trees, and he sat still, waiting for what would happen next.

I took his hand after he told me that, and I drew closer to him. Giving myself to a man might finally have a purpose, was the wish I was making. I'd been in love by then often enough to have noticed that my passion for any man coincided pretty neatly with the urgency of my need to escape my own character. I'd seen myself eat calamari, wear elaborate lingerie, claim to enjoy incoherent plays. Yet here was a man who had escaped himself long ago, on a clouded day in Burma, while trees fell around him and the ground grew supple and undulate. I don't think anyone who has ever wanted to feel the world as frankly as a stand of corn or a common bird would not have taken the chance I took.

We ended up in Chicago, where he had a friend who was storing a trunk for him. In that trunk was the money my husband had made during what he called his "invisible time." After high school he sent away for a book called *Your Right to Privacy*, which explained how to live outside government, how to remove your name from birth records and social security rolls. He lived for ten years like that, traveling the world, avoiding the draft and taxes, and after we were married we moved the trunk from his friend's apartment to ours.

"I feel criminal," I said, sitting next to him in the car that day, the trunk wedged into the back seat. I was remembering something my mother had said before we left Kansas City: You don't marry men like him, she told me. You carry their pictures in a locket. You keep their letters at the back of a lingerie drawer. "I feel like we're moving a body or something."

"Don't," he told me. "No one in the world knows about this money except you. If it makes you nervous, you only have to forget about it. That's about as gone as anything gets."

On that day, which was a cool summer day with a breeze off the lake, I looked out at the skyline of Chicago, the long towering line of apartment buildings that edged the shore. Still new to the city, I was moved by how many people lived there, and I felt a stranger to myself, like I could forget anything. He turned the radio on low and I rolled down the window. The breeze lifted my hair off my neck and then settled it again. I leaned back against the seat and closed my eyes. When I opened them again, we were home.

Even the baby was not a surprise. He wanted her, and after a childhood during which I'd been led to believe that even my good intentions could not save me, I wanted a baby who would grow up with him as father. While I was pregnant and full of extravagant feeling, I dreamed her—a rangy girl with tangled hair running over hills along the African coast, part of a graceful, long-legged herd of children that zagged toward the water like gazelles, then eased smoothly inland in a sudden shared choreography of will.

We named her Willa as a kind of testament to that dream. She was a long, lean, blonde baby with delicate fingers, quick eyes, and a serious mouth, and she was a baby of considerable will. From the day she was born she hated sleep. She'd struggle upright out of anyone's arms, bolt screaming out of sneaking dozes as if someone had thrown a blanket over her head. At some point we noticed that she closed her eyes easily only in clamorous and well-lighted public places—restaurants, el platforms, the Sunday afternoon beach—as if she needed hearty assurance of the world even as she slept. So nights at her bedtime we spread her quilt on the living-room floor, turned on all the lights and the TV, and talked over her until she drifted off.

One night, when Willa was thirteen months old and still struggling against being weaned, the three of us watched a documentary on the westernization of China. The insistent monotone of the interpreter's speech combined with the strange swallowed cadences of the Chinese seemed to please Willa in some way. She lay on her back, very still and alert, her eyes open, her thumb in her mouth. I could see that she was happy. Although she wasn't looking at me I smiled at her and then over my shoulder at my husband on the couch. He was watching the screen. He looked as happy as she did. "I've got to get there before I die," he said. My husband had been so many places in his life that he spoke of far off corners of the world the way I spoke of the dry cleaners down the block. "Just up the beach from Montevideo," he'd say, or "about a kilometer outside Toowoomba." Now he was a computer specialist, a systems troubleshooter for a huge corporation that sat far out in the suburbs on sixty acres of land, but China, open and in front of him, sat him up in his chair. He patted his pockets for his cigarettes and leaned toward the set.

"Watch this now. This is one of the world's last mysteries."

On the TV peasants swamped a group of American tourists shooting sixty-second film. The tourists shot their Polaroids frantically and tossed pictures into the crowd. There was a close-up of a man holding a snapshot of his child as it developed. His face reflected first a kind of simple, nodding good cheer, and then, as I imagined he began to recognize the features of his own child, a reverence. He pressed the snapshot to his chest and looked up into the filmmaker's camera. What his face showed then was gratitude.

"Look at that," I said. "Look at that face. It makes me want to go over there with whole crates of cameras."

"We'd become millionaires."

"Oh, not to sell," I told him. "I'd want to give it all to them."

He looked at me sharply. I thought perhaps Willa had stirred, but she was curled up now on the quilt, sleeping.

"What?"

He lit another cigarette, then threw the matchbook down. It skidded across the coffee table and fell to the rug.

"Nothing," he said. "I just hope that's your hormones talking. I hope that isn't you."

"Of course it's me." I stretched away from Willa to reach the matchbook. "Pay attention." I tossed the matches back at him. "I'm your wife."

He snatched the matchbook out of the air, slipped it in his pocket and smiled. "I recognize you," he said. "You're my wife, all right."

I looked back at the TV.

"Hey," he said until I turned around again. "All I meant is you can't just give things to people. You murder your own chances, and you murder theirs. Any good missionary will tell you that. Besides, what those people love about Americans is not all our stuff. What those people love about Americans is how we got all our stuff—buying and selling, putting our own needs first."

"Don't get all tough guy, citizen of the world with me. It's a TV show. We're watching TV."

"Right." He nodded and looked back at the TV, still smiling. "Let's do that."

I lay down next to Willa, who did stir then. She gave up her thumb and began to pull at my clothes, fretting to nurse. I slid her across my lap and patted her hard between the shoulder blades, which occasionally calmed her. Then I looked back at him.

"And don't talk to me about hormones when I'm weaning our child."

"Give me that baby. How can you expect her not to need you when you're right there next to her?"

I handed him Willa and he lay her on her back next to him on the couch, settling one hand on her chest. He didn't stroke her or pat her or try to ease her, and this benign neglect worked. She watched him for awhile, fiddled with his fingers, then found her thumb again. I looked back at the documentary. The interviewer was examining a farming couple on the nature of marriage. They sat before him in identical chairs, wearing almost identical clothing, and they appeared to be equally embarrassed by his curiosity.

"I'm wondering," the interviewer said, "what provokes marriage here. What sort of needs are fulfilled by it? Is it love, production, procreation?" The Chinese farmer cocked his head. He appeared actually to wince under the weight of this question, while his wife's uneasy smile grew more distant and fixed. I knew they weren't going to answer, but I sat up anyway and paid strict attention. Like the interviewer, I didn't know much about marriage. Even after three years with my husband I still had the sense I was making myself and the two of us up as I went along. The Chinese couple exchanged a quiet glance, and as I watched them some part of me held out hope that marriage meant two people resigned in good humor to their own poor characters. I realized then that I still believed in redemption, even for Americans, that someone or something might come along someday and show me my need by meeting it.

Not long after that night in front of the documentary my voice began to change. Willa noticed first, and it was the change in her behavior—her constant demands for me to talk to her, sing to her, tell her stories—that alerted my husband.

"Something's different," he told me one day at breakfast. "Your voice is younger—breathier or something. It's different somehow. She hears it."

I worried for the two weeks it took to get an appointment with my doctor, but when he saw me, he said I was okay, he said I was fine, it was only nodes—a lot of them, but benign. Then he referred me to a surgeon.

In the recovery room I woke to someone slapping my forearm.

"Open your eyes," she kept saying. "I need to hear your voice."

There was a slim possibility that my vocal cords, encrusted in the nodes, had been damaged, though I trusted the surgeon, a cancer specialist accustomed to far more delicate and tasking surgery than mine. I opened my eyes. The room was tiled white and cold as an icehouse. Suddenly a woman's face, fleshy and florid under her surgical cap, was above mine.

"Are you trying?" she asked. "You're not, are you?"

Under her gaze I felt puny and dissolute. I wanted to ask her for a blanket or something to make me sleep again, but I could hear how busy she was. I knew she wouldn't bring me anything, that she'd listen to me choke on a syllable, then disappear.

"I can see you're awake," she said, "and I'm going to stand here until you say something."

I closed my eyes then. I felt a deep, delicious stubbornness. A few days before I had taken Willa out to buy a new aquarium for her turtle. We were going to throw away the plastic thing with the miniature palm tree and do it right. At the pet store I shopped capably, choosing a modest, but spacious tank with a built-in sunning ledge, and Willa helped carry a bag of colored rocks up the steps to our apartment.

"Bobo is going to love all this," I told her. "He's going to stop feeling like a dime-store attraction. He's going to feel like a real turtle when we're done."

When I opened our front door I saw my husband kissing a girl who sometimes messengered his reports around his office complex. They were in the dining room. My husband had the girl pressed up against the table. Her back was arched and both his hands were involved in her long hair. I pushed Willa behind me.

"Okay," I said, "that should do it."

She was a raw-boned girl, with fleshy, full thighs and large breasts loose under her tee-shirt, but at the sound of my voice she straightened herself silkily. When she looked at me her eyes were still dreamy.

"Get out," I said. "You get out of my house."

My husband drew Willa from behind me and guided her down the hall and into her playroom. "Show Bobo his new pebbles," I heard him say. For a moment the girl and I were alone together. She stood still, not looking at me, then tucked her tee-shirt into her jeans. My husband came up the hall. He reached behind me to push the door closed, then stood between us.

"Do you want to sit down?" he asked. "Do you want to talk about this?"

I saw that he meant to create out of this chaos some sort of civilized and complicated event. I wouldn't have expected that from him. The girl relaxed at the sound of his voice. She drew her hair up in both her hands, then dropped it over her shoulders.

"Just try to be fair," she said.

I think even before she spoke I had decided that I could not bear to hear her voice in my house.

"You realize, don't you," I said to her, "that you're a lower form of life. That the damn houseplants are laughing at you."

She squinted at me. "Your husband doesn't seem to think so," she said.

We both looked at him. He put his hands in his pockets and shook his head lightly at the floor.

"I guess we can't be too sure of what my husband thinks, can we?"

She picked up her bag, a ridiculous cloth pouch held closed with a safety pin, from under the dining-room table.

"Well, I'm leaving," she said, looking my husband in the face as she passed him.

I reached behind me to pull the door open, but only enough so that she had to slide through. Then I eased my weight against it until I heard the click of the latch.

My husband and I looked at each other then in a new way, in the strange new light of my sudden authority.

"I'm sorry. It was stupid," he said. "It was unseemly. I've insulted you, and I'm sorry."

I pulled a chair away from the dining-room table and sat down. "I always thought you wouldn't lie. You might run off to Bogotá for six months, but you wouldn't lie."

"I'm not lying now, Nora. You know what she is. You nailed her. Don't pretend you don't know what happened here. Don't pretend you don't know how insignificant she is, because I'm not going to pretend she's more than that."

"I know what happened here," I said. I looked up at him. "I just want you to know there's going to be a problem for us now, and I'll tell you what that problem is going to be. That problem is going to be that I needed to believe that you would not do this, that you would never do this."

He sat down across from me, looked out into the living room for a time, and then back at me.

"I didn't ask you to believe that," he said. "I wouldn't have. You believed that on your own. If you'd asked me, I would have said, 'Never say never, Nora. One, it's sentimental. Two, it's dangerous. And three, it's always a lie.' "

In the recovery room it occurred to me that it might be useful to be mute. I have large expressive eyes. I could drive him mad, never offering him a word.

Outside an elevator, as the gurney on which I lay was rolled down a hallway and then nudged up against a wall, I woke to the scent of my husband's cigarettes and the wool of his good sports coat. Then I felt his presence next to me. He touched my hair and ran the back of his hand across my cheek—odd stylized gestures that I could not quite appraise. I kept my eyes closed. I thought of my mother. She had called the day before from Kansas City and asked to speak with my husband—something she had never in the three years of my marriage asked of me. I had told her about the girl, and so I hesitated.

"You're my only child," she said into the pause. "Now put that man on the telephone."

I held the receiver out to him.

"My mother," I said.

He spoke to her in clipped affirmatives. Yes, he would, he said. He knew that, he said. He was sure, he told her. Then he handed the phone back to me.

"He says he'll be there for you," my mother said. "Will he be there for you?"

"I think so," I told her.

"Well, I suppose this could be good. He should take care of you for awhile. He should remember his responsibilities." Slower then, with less certainty, she said, "I suppose this could be to your advantage."

"I suppose."

"So I won't come then."

"I guess not," I told her.

Next to my gurney my husband stood still. I knew he was staring down at me, though I did not open my eyes. I think I believed that my pain and deep fatigue would offer a clearer sense of the genuine than anything I might see.

"Your wife?" I heard a woman say.

"Yes."

"One of Dr. Scranton's patients?"

"Yes," my husband said again.

"So am I. So is half this ward," the woman said. "His work is a miracle, you know. Even the nurses say so. You keep that at the front of your mind now. You hold onto that."

I realized then that she believed I was a cancer patient, and in the quiet that followed her remark I knew my husband had realized that, too. I heard, in the silence, his confusion. It pleased me.

"She's very young," the woman said.

"She is." My husband paused again, and then he said, "We have a one-year-old daughter."

The woman gasped a little at this new and deepened sense of my tragedy. I came ferociously awake, feeling a little like Willa as I opened my eyes and startled them both away from me. The woman took a step back. My husband removed his hands from the side bar of my bed and put them in his pockets.

Two nurses came then and rolled my gurney into a room. They arranged rolled towels on either side of my neck to immobilize it, wrapped my sheet tight around me like a shroud, then slid me off the gurney onto a hospital bed. Over their heads I watched my husband hang back in a corner of the room. After they left he came to sit on the edge of the bed. He fingered a corner of the sheet, then folded it over the shoulder of my gown.

"The doctor said it went well. He wants you to try your voice."

"You son of a bitch," I mouthed at him.

He stood up from the bed, running both his hands through his hair, moving toward the door; then he turned back to me.

"What would you have said to her, Nora? 'My wife's not dying and I'm sorry if you are?' Is that what you would have said? For six hours," he pointed behind him to the door, "I have been sitting in a goddamn surgical waiting room." Leaning closer to me, he spoke through clenched teeth. "What is it you think people imagine in those rooms, Nora?"

I felt my eyes fill with tears and so I closed them.

After a time, he said, "I need to pick up Willa. I'll be back tomorrow."

I opened my eyes.

"After lunch," he said. He lay one hand on mine. "Try your voice, Nora."

I shook my head lightly.

Bending to kiss my forehead, he whispered, "All right then, don't."

After he left I wondered what sort of sin it was to imagine the death of your wife, and I wondered, Had he imagined my experience of it—the pain, the terrible slipping into loss—or only his own experience, only the absence?

Twice in my hospital bed I woke up confused. The first time I saw outside my window a low grove of trees on a grassy hillock, and I believed I was home, in Kansas City, in a downtown hospital where when I was sixteen I'd been kept in quarantine for scarlet fever. My mother had been allowed to visit me then only for a few nervous minutes each day, and since she wasn't at my bedside, the doctors must have felt they could speak their news directly to me. So they worried aloud—formally and gravely— over a weakening valve in one of the chambers of my heart. I had believed they meant I was dying. Outside my window then a narrow park rolled up another hill and on it sat a tower in memory of war dead. Sixteen years old, in my closed room, a window away from a sunny morning, I felt something more kindred than age and inequity with the boys memorialized by that tower. I felt the pure hollow loneliness of doom. That hospital had been a Catholic hospital, and each day, just after dawn, a priest came to my room wearing a surgical mask and carrying a chalice covered by a linen napkin. He touched my shoulder to wake me, and when I opened my eyes, he whispered, as if we were on sacred ground, "Child, would you like to receive the Holy Eucharist?" Each day I told him no.

The second time I woke to a swoon of pain as a woman I believed must be my mother removed a drain from the incision in my neck and then arranged a new dressing over the wound. She nursed me the way my mother had nursed me as a child—with a light tender touch that felt quickened by fear. I reached out for her hand, and she leaned close to whisper, "Don't move, honey. You don't want to feel how sick you'll be if you move." When she slid open the heavy drape I was confused by the sunlight. My mother had only touched me that way in the middle of the night, as if her love and dread ranged wilder in the darkness. Outside my window I saw the low trees again, and though this time I knew I wasn't home, the scene felt closer to home than I was, offered a promise, a contiguity. If I walked over that hill, and then kept walking, I could get there. I closed my eyes and slept.

When I woke again a woman stood in my doorway—the same woman who had spoken with my husband yesterday, the woman who believed I had cancer. Her face, anxious and tentative, still held the memory of what my husband had told her. I tried to raise myself in bed, but I moved too suddenly and a searing pain tore through my throat. Then, with horror, I felt the nausea the nurse had warned me about. I reached out to the woman in the doorway.

"I'm going to be sick," I said in a voice grainy and guttural, but familiar. Fingering the dressing over my throat, I said, "Oh my God, don't let me be sick."

The woman rushed to my bed and took my hand. "You won't," she said. "Lie very still. Breathe through your mouth. You won't be sick, dear. You won't be."

I did what she said and slowly the nausea subsided. I sank deeper into my pillows, exhausted then, and I closed my eyes. She stayed at my bedside, smoothing a blanket over my shoulders, gently pressing the rolled towels closer to my neck.

"I shouldn't have startled you." Her voice was low and hushed. "I only meant to peek in, say a good word." She patted my hand for a moment. "You're all right now, aren't you?"

I was just at the brink of sleep when she said it, but I felt myself called back lightly into consciousness—the way I'd felt since Willa was born, when I would linger briefly each night on the edge of sleep and wonder if I'd tuned her radio to an all-night station, latched her crib rail, done all that I needed to do for her. I opened my eyes and saw that she was an older woman with thinning, frowsy hair and a kind face, an earnest face. She still held my hand in hers.

"I'm not really dying," I whispered to her.

"Oh, of course you're not, dear." She squeezed my hand firmly between both of hers. "Of course you're not," she said.

After Rosa Parks

―――――――

Ellie found her son in the school nurse's office, laid out on a leatherette fainting couch like some child gothic, his shoes off, his arms crossed over his chest, his face turned to the wall.

"What's the deal, Kid Cody?"

When he heard her voice, he turned only his head toward her, slowly, as if he were beyond surprise. "I have a stomach-ache," he said.

"Yeah?" Ellie sat down beside him and stroked his bare arm.

"That's the message I got."

"It's a nervous stomachache, Mom. It's right in the middle."

He pointed to his belt buckle, a nicked metal casting of a race car. "It's right where Mrs. Schumacher said my nerves are."

Cody was in kindergarten, and he did not like school. He told anyone who would listen that he did not like school. Yesterday, from just inside their back door, Ellie overheard him telling their next-door neighbor Mrs. Schumacher that school gave him a bad feeling behind his stomach, "the kind of feeling," he said, "that you get before something happens." Ellie stood still in the doorway and watched as Mrs. Schumacher looked up from grooming one of her half dozen cats. Mrs. Schumacher was a stringy wild-haired widow—dirt poor, bone thin, and half-crazy with loneliness and neglect. Sometimes when Cody and Ellie would haul trash back to the cans in the alley, she'd wave and call out her kitchen window to Ellie, "You pull those shoulders back, girl. Divorce is no sin." Yesterday she picked cat hair out of a long metal comb and told Cody, "There are two kinds of stomachaches, you know. Now a sick one just swirls through your gut like a bad wind, but a nervous one sits real still." She pressed one gnarled hand to Cody's belly. "Almost like you've swallowed a baseball," she said. "And it glows."

"That's the one I get at school," Cody told her. "That's the one."

After he said it Ellie pressed her head against the cool storm door and felt sorry for herself, sorry she lived in the only rundown pocket of this suburb on probably the only street for miles where a woman could put her hands on her child and tell him such things.

The school nurse, a young red-haired woman strangely overdressed in a carnation pink suit, came from behind her desk to the couch. Ellie leaned back as the nurse ran her hand over Cody's forehead. "He doesn't have a fever as far as I can tell. But he won't take the thermometer in his mouth. He says he wants it under the arm."

"Axillary," Ellie said. "That's how we do it at home."

Cody lay still under the nurse's hand. "I told her that," he said.

"Well, at school we do it by mouth," the nurse said. "You need to try doing it that way at home so it won't be new at school."

Cody and Ellie both looked at the nurse, then Cody looked back at the ceiling. "It's a nervous stomachache, Mom," he said softly. "I can tell."

"Let's sit up, Cody," Ellie said. "You look sicker than you are like that, and lying down is not what you need. A break is what you need. Put your shoes on now."

Ellie stood up and took the nurse's elbow, led her to a window that looked out over an empty play yard. "He gets nervous," she said quietly. "It seems to happen most often when too many people treat him like a child."

The nurse looked at her.

"I mean when too many people try to tell him what to do," Ellie said. "See, he's an only child, and he lives half his time with his dad in their house and half his time with me in ours. So he's accustomed to partnership, you know, to being a partner in his own management. I mean, you live alone with a child, and there's none of that usual 'us versus him' kind of thing. You live alone with a child, and he's part of the us."

"Oh," the nurse said. She took a step back. People often did that when they learned how Cody lived. A social worker, new to their city from California, had concocted the scheme during the divorce. To Ellie and her ex-husband it had sounded humane, but Ellie and her ex-husband did not live in California. They lived in an old and mostly refined Midwestern suburb, a place where tall trees and wide driveways led back behind big houses to double and triple garages.

"I'm wondering," the nurse said, "if I have the correct home phone number for you. A man took the message when I called." She looked Ellie in the eye, insinuating now. "I think I woke him up."

"That's my brother. He's been staying with us to help out." Disappointed in herself for revealing more of their life than was necessary to this woman, Ellie added, "I'm sure you did wake him up. He's ill today."

Cody looked up from struggling with his shoelaces. "Uncle Frank is a night person," he said. "When I'm asleep, he's awake. He does life the opposite."

Ellie smiled at him and looked back at the nurse. "Frank works nights, is what he means."

The nurse's face said that even this fact made her suspicious.

"Look, I think Cody just needs extra time is all," Ellie said. "This is his first year of school. He didn't go the play group and preschool route. His father and I kept him home so he could get wise to both of us still being there for him, even though it was in different houses. He's fine about that, but he's no wise guy when it comes to school. Are you, Cody?"

Cody stood up and smiled. "I get stomachaches," he said. Both his shoes tied, he was ready to go now. Ellie saw that he believed the hard part of this day was behind him. Next to her the nurse narrowed her eyes at his sudden good humor, and Ellie felt her hesitate, weighing for a moment whether Cody was a liar or only a new and distinct form of damaged child. Then she looked at Ellie, and Ellie saw that what the nurse had decided was that Cody was an odd child, that he was an ill-equipped child—a child with a strange and probably damaged life—and probably, Ellie understood the nurse was thinking, probably it was Ellie's fault. They stared at each other a moment. Then Ellie went to Cody and took his hand.

"I'll just take him now. We'll be on our way. We'll try school again tomorrow, right, Cody?"

"Okay," he said.

"You have to sign him out." The nurse pointed to a binder on her desk. "For our records."

"Right," Ellie said. "No problem."

They drove slowly away from the school. Cody rolled the window down and rested his head on the door frame so that the wind lifted his hair off his forehead. Ellie didn't know if he was pensive or only relieved. Maybe he had sensed what the nurse thought of her. Or of him. She turned the radio on low.

"Do you want to drive by the lake?" she asked. "It's warm today. We could climb down the rocks to the beach."

The beach was where Cody told Ellie things, where he confided in her. The wide expanse of sand and water loosened something in him. It was there, digging a hole one day last spring with a new miniature folding spade, that he had looked up and said, "Do you want to hear something secret?"

"Sure," Ellie told him, and then he recited, nearly word for word, an ugly desperate argument she and her ex-husband had had just before they gave it all up. He recited it so precisely that the night came back to Ellie. She'd made a formal dinner in the middle of the week—cornish hens stuffed with herbs and rice. A friendly Greek man at the liquor store had helped her choose a nice wine that she served in their wedding crystal. She'd left the bottle on the table, tucked in a hammered silver ice bucket, while she and her ex-husband said horrible, hurtful things they'd never said before or since. On the beach that day, Cody recited it all. He paused in his digging and looked up at her. "I was under the table," he said. "You just didn't see me there."

For a moment Ellie believed him. Then she remembered another moment, carrying their salad plates to the kitchen, when she'd been so ashamed she'd gone back to Cody's room to check on him. He lay sideways in his youthbed, one foot wedged between the bars. From the doorway she listened to his breathing before she went to his bed and straightened him, sliding his foot from the bars, folding his quilt up over his shoulders. On the beach she felt the same relief she'd felt at his door. He'd been asleep. He'd slept through it. She watched him dig the hole, throwing sand over his shoulder, hunkering down to his work, and suddenly she was shaken again.

"Daddy didn't tell you those things, did he? Did Daddy tell you those things?"

"No." He looked up from his digging, a little wary of her.

"Oh."

"Daddy says I probably dreamed it."

They were both quiet then. He finished his hole and sat back on his heels to admire it. It was deep, the deepest he'd dug, and he fingered his new shovel lightly. Then he crawled into the hole, tucking his legs up to his chest and folding his arms around them. "Cover me up, Mom," he said, smiling then.

She slid the warm sand over him as he watched her. When the sand covered the tops of his knees, she smoothed it around his chest. He looked up at her.

"I did see it," he said.

She took her hands away from him and sat back.

"I know," she said. "I know you did."

Now, in the car, she looked at him. "How about it?" she asked.

"No, thanks. I don't feel like the beach."

"We could try the library."

"No," he said. "Thanks."

"Well, I need a milk shake. I'm going to pull into that hot dog stand under the train tracks and have a chocolate shake."

He didn't answer, but Ellie pulled in anyway and settled him outside under a striped umbrella, where she brought his milk shake out to him. He drank it quickly, tipping his head back, while Ellie looked up at the train platform where a few late commuters stood next to their briefcases. She was glad now she and Cody were not going anywhere, glad she had taken the rest of the day off when she got the call at the office, glad they could sit here half the morning and then stop at the park if they felt like it. The gift of her child was that in his presence life lengthened and uncoiled. Although it was nearly eleven o'clock, this day spread out before them as sweetly as at dawn.

"I like ice cream in the morning," Cody said. "This is the first time I've had ice cream this early."

"It's a quiet pleasure," Ellie said. "That and the weather. This is the warmest January we've ever had, I think."

"I remembered this was your day," Cody said. "So I told her to call you and not Dad."

Ellie touched his wrist. "You were right. Exactly right. You're getting very good at this. You're becoming a big boy."

Cody looked out over the parking lot. The umbrellas rippled in the breeze like sails, and above them the late commuters swayed lightly like distant buoys. "I would kick a bad guy in the stomach if he came near our table."

"That would do it," Ellie said.

"I'd karate kick him in the stomach and then in the knee."

"He'd go limping off to the other side of the world," Ellie said.

This was something new for them that had started with school—this imagined violence, her child's sense of himself as a warrior and her quiet affirmation. School had forced Ellie to see how divorce had changed her—that she had become a cautious person, a person who lived as if she were allowed only one mistake in life and had already made it—and school had forced her to see that she was sending her son off into the world with the rigid moral sense of a saint. He'd see a child steal another child's hat in the play yard, and he'd suffer it all day. When he came home he'd tell her the story of the theft and then lie on the rug, exhausted, looking up at her to say, "That was a terrible thing, don't you think, Mom? Don't you think that was an awful thing to do?"—as if he'd witnessed a murder. So now she let Cody talk this way, imagining his own power, and lately she had begun to surprise him with figures from a set of fierce dinosaurs and cavemen as a way of making up for all the early years she'd encouraged a pristine sensibility.

"Cody, did anything happen today, I mean before you went to the nurse with a stomachache?"

"No."

"Nothing?"

"Well, the playground lady made me take a time out."

"Why was that?"

"I was swinging on my belly."

"Uh-huh."

"And that's all." He rolled the edge of his cup around one finger. "There's a rule against swinging on your belly."

"I didn't know that."

"I didn't know that either, but the lady said that now I would know and now I would remember."

"Oh. Well, I guess she's the boss."

"She is."

Ellie ran her hand along the rough close-cropped hair at the nape of his neck. He looked away from her when she did it.

"So then what happened?"

"I had to sit on the ground by her feet for awhile and then I had to say I was sorry."

"Did you?"

"Yes."

"And then what?"

"Then she called me Cory and told me I could go."

"She called you by the wrong name."

"Uh-huh. Yes."

"Did you tell her?"

"No." He leaned against her then and tilted his head back to look into her face. "I didn't want her to know me by my right name, Mom."

She put one arm lightly around his shoulders and rested her chin on the top of his head.

"What should we do now?" she asked softly.

"Go home."

At home, Frank was on the couch, an afghan pulled over his legs, watching the noon news.

"You're awake early," Cody said.

Frank looked up. "You're home early."

Cody quieted when he said it. He dropped his knapsack under the hat rack, pulled out his box of dinosaurs and cavemen and began to arrange them delicately, as though he were being watched. Frank raised his eyebrows at Ellie. She shook her head.

"I guess I'll make soup or something," she said.

A few minutes later Frank joined her in the kitchen. He moved stiffly to the sink, leaned there a moment, then drew a glass of water from the tap and sat down at the table.

"It's vegetable soup." Ellie turned from the pot on the stove. "Can you tolerate it?"

"Not today." He raised his glass. "Today I'm drinking water." Frank suffered from colitis—at least that's what he said it was. He'd been a medic in the army and learned just enough about medicine to believe he could treat himself. Last week, though, he'd been so sick that Ellie had convinced him to let her drive him to the VA hospital for some tests. Nudged into a pocket of darkness between two high-rise office buildings, the hospital was a spooky place—cavernous and forbidding and full of old and middle-aged men shuffling the hallways in paper slippers.

"This is awful," Ellie whispered to Frank as they stood in some line. "Why don't you get real health insurance?"

"Forget it," Frank said. "I spent three years of my life defending the Golden Gate Bridge to earn this."

She noticed as he walked away from her that day, and again this morning as he came into the kitchen, that he had begun to look like those men at the VA. He'd begun to look like a damaged man. Although he was tall and thick with muscle he carried himself lightly, his arms held away from his body, as though he were hollow. Today his rumpled hair stood up from his head. Under each eye was a white translucent spot of pain.

"You look pale, Frank."

"I feel pale."

"Did you call for your test results?"

"They said they'd call me."

"You should check."

"They said they would call, Ellie."

She turned back to the stove and then called, "Soup in twenty minutes, Cody."

"And biscuits, please," he called back.

"Okay, and biscuits." She peered into the refrigerator, looking for the plastic container of dough.

"That is not a sick child," Frank said.

"He was nervous. Something happened on the playground."

Ellie went about her work quietly, spreading flour on the countertop, rolling out the dough, but she felt like Cody had looked a moment ago in the other room. She felt like she was being watched. Frank sat at the table, the glass of water between his broad hands. Her brother was an odd man. There was such power to him, in his hands and legs and the set of his jaw, but around other people—even Ellie and Cody—he was always quiet and watchful, slightly ill at ease. Ellie believed that life—real life, life in society, whatever it was she was living—was a confusion to Frank. She wasn't sure why. Sometimes she blamed the army. Frank had been one of the last men drafted into Vietnam. Although the war ended not long after he finished basic training, the army had changed him—perhaps in ways worse than a year fighting in the jungle might have changed him. She didn't know. She wasn't even sure exactly what he had done during those years or what had been done to him. Occasionally, he'd written to Ellie of demotions, restrictions, extra duty, a few short stays in the brig. She had tried to imagine what circumstances could have landed her brother in a military jail, in a cage. As a boy he had been cocksure and strong-willed, and sometimes he'd had a smart mouth, but all boys had seemed like that to Ellie back then.

When the war ended Frank wrote to say that he was glad, but for an odd reason. If he'd gone to war, he'd written, his resistance might have become inflated even in his own mind into some kind of grand refusal. He might have gone the rest of his life thinking that what he had learned was that he could not kill anyone or that a big country should keep its nose out of a little country's affairs. Then he would have missed what he said was the only real lesson of the army, which was that people who tell you what to do—no matter what reasons they claim—are performing an act of aggression. You're in their way, is what Frank had written to her; they'd just as soon you die.

When he was discharged, he roamed the world—Ellie imagined he roamed it with that credo—crewing sailboats to New Zealand, working illegal shrimp boats out of Key West, leading tourists across the Yucatán Peninsula. For fifteen years he lived like that, never settling long enough for anyone or anything to impose itself upon him. That he came when she needed him had surprised her—though both their parents had died and there was no one else to help her. Frank spotted her first at the airport, and when she recognized him it was by the easy certain smile she remembered. When she came close, though, he stepped lightly away from her. He shook her hand first and then he shook Cody's.

The nature of his support was also a surprise. He said very little, never entered into the acrimony of her divorce, never said more to her son than a benevolent stranger might say. He simply sat nearby while she found a job, a place to live, a car, while she went about the business of solving her life, and each Saturday morning, on the hall stand outside her bedroom door, he left two one-hundred dollar bills folded under an old candy dish of their mother's.

Only once, just after he arrived, while they sat next to each other on a commuter train bringing them back from the court-room where she had been ordered to sell her home, had he spoken up.

"You're getting screwed," he told her.

"I know."

"You're just standing there letting it happen."

"It's worse if you make a fuss. I tried that once and even my own attorney yelled at me. You're just supposed to stand there and take it. It's all a glorified trip to the principal's office." She looked out the window when she said it.

"You're nuts. You're only seeing what's in front of you." When she didn't turn around he leaned closer to her and lowered his voice. "For what you'll end up paying that lawyer we could buy a little guest camp I once stayed at in Bali. It's real popular with the Australians, but far enough away that you'd never be found. Cody could grow up knowing how to catch his own dinner."

Still looking out the window she considered it. She could take a few books, a bag of mementos, and her son, and disappear into a tropical life of light, loose clothing, modest shelter, balmy breezes. She turned to Frank. Perhaps this was how he had solved his life—not so much by running away from danger as by following closely the slender path of peace.

"It's against the law," she said.

He shook his head. "If you're not careful, that's the law you're going to leave your kid. You have a choice, you know."

Ellie looked out the window again. Maybe she had never known she had a choice. She was a woman, a divorced mother of a young child. For a long time her life had been one of necessity and ultimatum, not choice. But Frank was different, and she realized that his time in the army most likely marked the beginning of a deal he'd struck with himself, because since those years ended she could not name one thing he had done that he had not chosen to do. She turned to face him again.

"I can't do it, Frank."

He looked at her then with the same expression she had seen flash over him in the courtroom earlier that day. His face became quizzical as an aborigine's. As he settled back into his seat and looked past her at the city dimming into twilight she saw something else, too. She saw his resignation. Never would they live together in a tropical guest camp. She had slipped, somehow, away from him. She felt that loss carve out a hole next to the loss of her marriage, her home, the life she had believed would be hers and her son's, and she felt the nature of Frank's love for her, and of hers for him, change from hope to regret.

Moved suddenly at this memory she sat down with him at the kitchen table. She felt tears behind her eyes and pressed the palms of her hands against them.

"What?" Frank said.

"Nothing. I don't know. Maybe I should talk with his dad. We could put him in a different school, I guess."

"All schools are the same." Frank placed his thick hands flat on the table and looked at them. "They're the same man in a different hat."

"Maybe he'll get used to it. Maybe it just takes time."

Frank took a small sip of water and then glanced to the pot of soup, which was boiling too fast on the stove. "Look," he said, "why don't you go back to work? I'll watch him. You can work late and make up the hours. He and I'll walk up to the chicken place for dinner and then I'll get him to bed."

She looked at him, suddenly tired, but acquiescent, too.

"Go on," he said.

———

She worked until past nine that night, leaving for home when lightning from a sudden thunderstorm flickered the lamp at her desk. On the drive home the rain turned to a fraudulent snow— huge wet flakes out of a sentimental movie. She could still hear thunder out over the lake, though, rumbling distantly like doom, and she leaned over the steering wheel, anxious to be home. More and more lately the thought came to her that in all the world she had only two blood relatives. In the company of that fact she felt skittish and threatened, as if two blood relatives were too slender a tie to bind her to the world.

The front of the house was dark except for the flicker of the TV in the living room. Frank was asleep on the couch, his breathing ragged and shallow. She stopped to turn off the TV and then saw the slant of light from Cody's doorway down the hall.

"Hey," she said.

He was sitting up in bed with a big book open in his lap. "Uncle Frank felt sick so I'm reading my own night story."

She came to sit beside him. "That was good of you. But it's late. Lights out."

"We went to Chicken in a Basket and I got a Coke. A large. That's why I'm so awake."

"Still." She closed his book and slid him down so that his head settled on his pillow.

"I saw the snow. Is that why you're late?"

"I worked extra so I could take you to story hour at the library tomorrow."

"Oh," he said, already drifting off. Then he opened his eyes. "After dinner we watched the freak feature on TV. It was about giant ants that hide in the sewer. Have you seen that one?"

"I think so. It's a scary one. Don't tell about it now. You'll have bad dreams. Tell about it in the morning."

He closed his eyes again and rolled on his side to sleep. She stroked his hair off his forehead, and he took her hand and tucked it under his chin. Without opening his eyes, he said, "I'm going to tell Daddy, too, when I see him, and I'm going to find out if they have that giant ant movie at the movie store so he can watch it, too."

"You're full of plans," she said, leaning down to kiss him. Before she sat up again he was asleep, and he had let go of her hand.

In the kitchen she gathered their paper cups and the boxes of chicken bones. At the trash can she stopped, holding the lid open with one hand, and stared at four empty beer cans. Drinking was something Frank had chosen not to do in her home. He never used the word *alcoholism*, but he had asked her when he moved in not to keep liquor in the house. "It distracts me," he told her. For the first month or so of his time with them he drank a lot of everything else—water, soft drinks, iced tea—and he slept a lot. Occasionally, too, he took long hushed phone calls from men Ellie believed must belong to AA or some support group—

extremely polite, low-voiced men, men she thought of as veterans of another kind. She closed the lid of the trash can and moved to stand by the sink, still holding the chicken boxes and paper cups.

Frank came in then from the living room. "What's up?" he asked when he saw her face. "Is Cody okay?"

She set the trash back on the kitchen table. "You drank."

"I know."

"Well, why? I mean, what am I supposed to do now, Frank? Am I supposed to kick you out?"

"You're not supposed to kick me out. Jesus, Ellie. You're supposed to drive me downtown to detox or something."

She sat down at the table, the vision of those men in paper slippers at the VA clanging around in her head. Frank filled a tall glass with water from the tap and sat down across from her. When she looked at him he straightened his spine and set his shoulders, but his eyes drifted unsteadily. He lowered his head.

"What's going on?" she asked.

"The VA called."

"What is it? Is it colitis?"

"A long time ago it was probably colitis." He looked at her. "Now it's cancer, Ellie."

She put her hand on his. He leaned back in his chair and she felt his privacy, his strict isolation. His hand was still on the table beneath hers. It did not seem fair that he be forced to suffer more isolation. "I'm sorry," she said, and took her hand away.

He shook his head. "It gets worse," he said, smiling lightly. "They went ahead and scheduled me for more tests and then this clerk called back and told me I don't qualify for treatment. 'This is not a service-related ailment,' he told me. 'The VA treats only the indigent and service-related ailments.'"

"You didn't know that?" she asked softly.

He rubbed his temples with both hands and pushed his hair roughly away from his face. "No."

"So what this means," she began slowly.

"What this means is I have cancer and no health insurance."

She sat back in her chair, stunned by the precision of this cruelty. Her brother had stepped off a plane just over a year ago tanned and strong, his only weakness being that he would not keep track of rules. He had balked even when she suggested he get a driver's license. She closed her eyes at the memory. She was the reason he'd come back to this place where his weakness could turn on him so cruelly.

"We'll figure it out, Frank. We'll figure something out."

"No. No. I've already done that. I just hate to leave you in a bind. I've got a little money I was saving to go back to Negril this spring. I'll leave you some of it and still make out pretty well there myself."

"What are you saying?"

"I'm saying I'm going to Negril." He looked sad for her when he said it, as if he believed she were the one with the greater loss. "I'll leave in a couple days."

"Frank, my God. You have to take care of this. You can't just walk away from it."

"I'm not walking away, Ellie. There are doctors in Negril. I'm not saying I won't take care of it. I'm just saying I can't take care of it here."

He was lying, she thought. He had decided somehow that to die whole on ground he understood would be better than struggling here. She sat rigidly across from him, her mind wildly in search of hope, of a kindly Jamaican doctor down there who would take Frank in and cure him for no more reward than the satisfaction of having preserved such a man. But she had never met a doctor like that. She wasn't sure the world was a place large and varied enough to hold even one doctor like that.

"How can I stop you," she said, "from doing this?"

"You can't." He pushed back his chair and stood up. "I'm tired, Ellie. I'm going to go to bed now."

He didn't go to bed. For hours she heard his silence as he moved through rooms. She wondered if perhaps he was saying good-bye to the house, to its small comforts, but then she understood that he no longer saw her home as a safe place. She was frightened for herself, knowing that. He stood in the kitchen a long time, the house so quiet around him she felt she could hear his resolve building. Then he went into Cody's room. She sat up in bed and put one foot on the floor, listening until he came out again.

When she opened her eyes next, Cody stood at her bedside.

"Is it morning?" he asked.

She looked to the window. Outside the snow was gone and the sun shone brightly.

"Yes."

"I had a bad dream. I had a dream someone got into our house."

"Uncle Frank was up late last night. You probably heard Uncle Frank."

"I dreamed it was someone else."

"It wasn't," she said. "It was Uncle Frank."

They washed and dressed hurriedly, though it was still early. Ellie let Cody watch cartoons as he ate, grateful for the noise and distraction. As they were leaving she lingered in the quiet front room, looking down the hallway to Frank's closed door. Cody stood in his coat and hat, watching her.

"Let's go now." She took his hand. "Time to go."

They arrived early at Cody's school, and his teacher looked up from a table in the back of the room, but she came to greet them in the hallway.

"A new day and a new start," she said merrily.

Cody reached up to hold onto a corner of Ellie's jacket.

"Today the Green Star group is going to spend the morning at the sand table," his teacher said to him. "Why don't you hang up your coat and get started?" She looked to Ellie. "Cody is in the Green Star group."

Ellie nodded.

"I have to tell my mom something," Cody said.

"Well, hurry along. We don't want to make Mom late for work or whatever."

"Okay," Cody said, and then stood mute next to Ellie, still clutching her jacket. His teacher watched him for a moment and then went back into the classroom.

"Hurry along," she called. "I'll take the top off the sand table."

Cody stiffened and began to cry as Ellie slipped his coat off his shoulders. She took his hands, warm with the moist heat of emotion and fear.

"What is it you want to tell me, Cody?"

He shook his head, his eyes a little desperate and lost.

"You don't know what it is?"

He shook his head again.

She nodded and pulled him close. "I love you, child," she said into his ear. Then she drew him away from her. "I think you can do this. I think it's important that you do this." He wouldn't look at her when she said it.

———

Pulling up to the school that afternoon she saw his face at the door, a bobbing pale moon in the glass that drew an ache up from her own stomach, but he ran down the slope to her car like the other children, trailing his knapsack behind him.

"Did it go okay?"

"Yeah." He closed his door, locked it, and drew the seat belt around him. "At the bad parts, I just pretended I was somewhere else. I pretended it wasn't really happening."

They were early to story hour and Cody hovered near the librarian at her desk, telling her the story of the giant ant movie he had seen. She was a kind older woman, wise in the ways of children, and she listened raptly to Cody's story, then led him off to a far corner of the children's room. Ellie sat with their coats in a small low chair and watched the other mothers and children arrive. A few minutes later Cody came running back carrying some books the librarian had found for him. They were junior novelizations of old monster movies: *The Mummy, Frankenstein,* and *King Kong.*

"Oh, these are too scary for you, Cody. These things even give me the willies."

"Mom," he said. "She gave them to me. I was going to show them to Uncle Frank."

"Oh. Well, let me see." She flipped the pages while he leaned against her shoulder. Mainly they were just a collection of black-and-white stills from the old movies.

"Maybe they give you the willies because the monsters are always after a lady." Cody pointed to a picture of the Mummy carrying a woman into a dark wood.

"Maybe," she said, closing the book. "I don't know."

"Could I show them to Uncle Frank? They won't scare him, I bet."

"Sure," she said. "I guess."

He crawled into her lap then, and Ellie watched the preparations for story hour while Cody paged through his books.

"I read the sign," Ellie said. "Today is a special puppet show for Martin Luther King's birthday."

"Our teacher told us about him in school."

"I'm glad. He was a good brave man."

"Once nothing was fair for brown-skinned people."

"Martin Luther King changed some of that, though."

Cody turned around and looked at her. "He got killed," he said.

"I know. I was a girl. It was very sad."

Cody leaned back against her then and fingered his monster books. His body grew slack against hers, and she thought he must be tired, but then she felt heat move out of him, the same heat she had felt in his hands that morning. She turned him around in her lap.

"What's wrong, Cody?"

He shook his head and she remembered this morning, how he had wanted to tell her something he didn't know.

"What is it?"

"Don't tell Daddy," he said.

He had never spoken those words to her before. Perhaps because of the way he lived or perhaps because of his own good nature Cody had always been unstintingly fair in his attachments to each of his parents.

"I don't know," Ellie said. "Why not Daddy?"

"It's not a man's secret."

"It's a woman's secret?"

"Uh-huh. I think so."

"What is it?"

"I'm afraid about dying. Do you just fall down one day and then it hurts forever?"

After he said it she pulled him close. Children did this, she had read somewhere, picked up the unspoken cues and terror in their homes.

"It doesn't hurt," she told him. "It stops all the hurt."

She drew her hand across his forehead.

"It feels like this," she said.

She knew when she said it that something was terribly wrong with her. To portray death to her own child as more dignified and easeful than life was some sort of abomination larger than she could fathom. But she did not take it back. She rocked Cody gently as the librarian rang a small bell and called for the children to gather around the puppet theater. She sat blankly, Cody curled against her, as the show began with a cardboard cut-out of a strictly segregated bus—a cluster of white circles at the front, a cluster of black circles at the back. *Before Rosa Parks*, the caption under the bus read. Then the librarian explained to the children that Rosa Parks was tired and believed she had as much right to sit down and rest as anyone else.

It's a woman's secret, Ellie thought. This was what her son believed. How he must have wondered to find a woman's secret in his own mind, to understand that to the teeming power and circumstance of the world he would lose many things—one day even his life. Cody's head lolled against her shoulder. She realized he was asleep in her arms. The monster books slid out of his hands and she held them a moment, looking into the shy pain on King Kong's face. She shook Cody lightly.

"We have to go," she said. "We have to hurry."

At home, Frank was on the couch watching the news. He smiled briefly when they came in, then looked back at the television. Cody ran to him with the monster books. He wanted Frank to read them to him.

"In one minute," Frank said. "When the news is over I'll read all three."

While Ellie hung up their coats Cody eased himself onto the couch and sat stiffly next to Frank, thumping his feet against the cushion. Frank lay one hand on his knee to quiet him. An old newsreel of Martin Luther King's last speech was playing on the TV.

"I saw him at the library," Cody said. "A picture of him. It's his birthday."

"Monday," Frank said.

"My friend Bennie's dad is off work Monday, and Bennie doesn't have school, but I do."

"How come you have school? I thought everyone was off," Frank said. "It's a holiday."

Cody was quiet then, and Ellie saw that he was a little teary, blinking and looking away from Frank to the TV.

"I don't know," he said. "I just do."

Frank shook Cody's knee gently. "Well, that stinks," he said, smiling. "That's not fair." He shook his knee more roughly until Cody began to smile, too, and then he leaned close to him.

"Just don't go," Frank said. "Stay home."

Cody looked at him. Ellie could see that Cody had not considered that an option before, that he had never completely understood he had an option, and next she knew he was going to look to her. She turned away quickly to the front window, afraid to watch the idea of freedom dawn in her son's face, but outside in the evening sky growing up at the end of her block, she saw it anyway—the sudden knowledge loose in his mind, spreading like the shadows that spilled from under stoops, crawled across lawns, and bloomed up from the dark center of even her own scraggly hedgerow. Her son was free. Behind her, music signaled the end of the news. It was late. She knew she should turn around, start dinner, but she stood a moment longer, staring out at the dark, and felt rising in her own mind the strangest and most fearsome comfort.

Who
Knows
More
Than
You

Although it was Saturday my sister Bette
called early, just after I heard the paper hit the front step.
"Hold on a minute," she said when I answered, and I heard her
call out to her daughter to pick up the baby's bottle.

"He threw it under the highchair. No, just set it on the tray.
Honey, he doesn't like you to hold it for him anymore. There,
that's what he wants," I heard her say.

Because we shared a childhood and parents so intricately
spooky that one lifetime, Bette liked to say, wasn't long enough
for successful therapy—if we believed in such a thing, I liked
to add—Bette called herself a self-taught mother. To me, her

older sister, as frightened by the idea of children as I was by therapy, she said it was easier than it sounded. "You just perform the opposite of every parental gesture you ever witnessed."

That was as close as we came to discussing the past. A long time ago we stopped speaking its specifics. Instead, nearly every weekday, sometime during the hour between when she got home from work and her husband did, Bette phoned while the kids bathed or had supper, talking as much to them as she did to me. I felt right there with her, and the benign sounds of her life, the children splashing or banging spoons, spoke as clearly as words. She was okay now, and maybe, she meant to say, I was, too.

Then, two days ago, I listened as her daughter Belinda, nearly five, sassy and smart as a monkey, refused three times to sit down at the kitchen table for supper.

"I'm going to count," Bette said. "Now apply yourself to that chair."

"Your mother means business," I heard Bette's husband say. He must have just walked in the door.

"What's she doing?" I was whispering, as if Belinda could hear.

Into the phone, Bette whispered back, "It appears she's considering the idea." Louder, to Belinda, she called, "Don't think right now, sweetie. Just do."

A moment later Belinda cried out in what I recognized even on the phone as real pain.

"Give her to me," Bette shouted, and then, low into the phone, she said, "Jesus." She repeated it, this time as if she'd been punched between the shoulder blades. The word came out like a cough. "Jesus. Those are bruises. Someone has struck my child," she said, and then she hung up.

Born after Bette spent two months on her back to stave off premature labor, Belinda grew up a cause for celebration. Weeks after she walked, people still applauded her, so tiny and birdlike a girl that common milestones rose to triumphant. Bette's great relief framed every moment of that child's life, and inside it, Belinda had so far grown first beautiful, then stubborn, then precocious, and then sure.

The last time they visited I held her on my lap in the front car of the el train through five or six stops while she chatted me up about who did I think threw that trash on the tracks and which tall buildings had I been in and did I know why that man wore no shoelaces in his shoes. Then she leaned against me, fiddling with my fingers as the train lulled on. With her head under my chin, legs lined up over mine, I felt ease in our connection, and for the first time wondered what it would be like to know her as a woman. Perhaps, her body so close to mine, she felt what I was feeling, because she pressed my hand gently in hers, then turned and said, I thought a little sadly, "You know, you are not the boss of me."

It startled me to silence, a child that certain of who she was and where she belonged.

"Was that a bad thing to say?" she asked.

"Oh no," I told her. "No, actually, you're right."

"But was it un*u*sual?" She looked truly bothered by that word. "Was it a too un*u*sual thing to say?"

It came to me, after Bette hung up, that the person who had taught Belinda to pronounce that word with such distaste was the same person who'd hit her hard enough to leave a bruise.

Penny did it, I found out when Bette called back.

"It's okay if you worried it might have been me," Bette said. "I was so crazy at first, even I wondered if I'd done it."

"Oh please." Always Bette moved too quickly into guilt. A vase crashing in another room could set her rigid for long seconds examining her conscience before she remembered she owned a cat. "Would you have a second thought?" I asked. "You did not do this."

"No," she said. "But someone did."

Penny was the babysitter, a neighbor of Bette's husband's parents. "A jewel," was how they described her, "A quiet, modest woman who'd quit work years ago to raise six well-behaved children of her own." Although we'd never met I'd imagined an ordinary hard-working woman who went to church and set the table and perhaps still ironed clothes. I'd never considered what it might mean to charge such a woman with the care of a child who'd been raised to believe herself extraordinary.

This morning Bette called so early because she had an insight. "The problem with people like us," she said, "is not that we think all the fresh-faced, smiling, well brought up people *aren't* what they appear to be. Oh no, the problem is we think they *are*. That's the problem." She paused and I heard water running, dishes knocking around the sink. "I'm sorry," she said. "I shouldn't have said us. I didn't mean you."

The bottom had fallen out of her voice. She sounded like the child she'd once been, a bereft and frightened girl who had to be led by the hand. Even after a year of school she clung to me every morning as we neared her classroom door.

"I may have forgotten my pencil," she'd say. "I'm pretty sure, really, that I left without my pencil."

A teacher would have to come and pry her away.

Somehow, and with no more care than a person might extend to a dog chained in the yard, Bette managed to grow from that trembling child into a tough bad girl and then into a woman who one day out of the blue married a nice man and moved with him to the distant suburbs of a smaller, less brutal city than the one where we were raised. The sudden drop in her voice alarmed me. I worried that if Bette lost her grip she might slide all the way back to her beginnings.

"Don't do that," I said. "We're not so different, Bette."

Although we'd each made a life for ourselves that the other either didn't or couldn't imagine we pretended we hadn't. She had one of those living rooms no one sat in and a family room off the kitchen and a playroom in the basement for the kids, and I paid more than their monthly mortgage to rent the first floor of a crumbling two-flat next to the elevated tracks in the city she fled. We just left it alone. When she visited me, she didn't mention the rat bait near the dumpster or the first 5 A.M. train that shuddered the building, and when I visited her, loading and unloading the kids on a series of errands at tidy chain stores, I didn't mention that every car in every parking lot looked new or that all the people were white or that we couldn't find food that wasn't advertised on TV. I assumed Bette felt for me what I felt one day for her, when, sitting next to her at a stoplight, the kids buckled in behind us, I found myself suddenly near tears. Nothing had happened to justify such outsized emotion—we'd only been to a children's shoe store and then a drive-through for lunch—but something leaned me back against the car seat, pressed my lips together, and closed my eyes. In that humming darkness I thought dumbly, as if I'd discovered a feeling so new I needed to name it, this must be hope.

"Twenty-five years I spent on red alert before I relaxed," Bette said. "Always certain the worst could happen. And I get blind-sided by a woman named Penny. How can that be? I haven't just been missing something," she said, "I've been missing a lot."

"Talk to me about Belinda," I said.

"I don't know." She lowered her voice. "In bed last night she talked for two hours. Awful stories. They were awful stories." Then she said, "Listen, I think I'm not going to tell you what she told me, okay? If someday maybe she decides to tell you, that's fine, but I don't think I should, okay?"

"That's fine," I said. "Okay."

I listened to a silence during which she swallowed more than once.

"Bette," I said, "I am so sorry."

"Don't you dare. Don't you dare be sorry. Belinda is going to be all right. You're my sister," she reminded me. "Don't you dare forget what I know that could help that child."

"I won't," I said, and throughout the morning, I didn't. I turned the pages of the *Times*, one after the other, not reading, but re-minding myself of what my sister knew, which was nobody's business but hers and, today, mine. To close my eyes on the present dropped me down a well, but I did it for my sister. Glimpses of things I never wanted to see and didn't want to see again flashed on, and I considered them until a clammy dark feeling rose up and eclipsed all. Distantly, the heat clicked on in the basement, and I turned at the dry rush of air through the register, startled by a sound like breath. Outside my window the flowering cherry tree, which bloomed the week before, its petals blanketing the shade garden like snow, was a relief. I fixed on it, understanding

I would need many of the days ahead, if not to forget what Bette knew, then to remove it, at least, from plain sight.

Around ten the phone rang again. It was my friend Walter calling from his old neighborhood, two train stops past mine, where he'd driven to drop his son off at his ex-wife's for the weekend. Walter and his son lived out in the country now, just over the state line, with trees and yards and houses a normal person could afford. He rarely got back to town, and when I asked why he didn't just drive over, he said something I couldn't hear over the sound of a passing train.

"Sorry," he said when it had passed.

"Where's Roy?" I asked, meaning his son. Walter was a sweet, distracted man I'd watched forget his briefcase three times on the way out of one room, and that train sounded close.

"No, I've got him sitting on a bus bench. I can see him from here. I just had to phone you."

For ten years Walter and I had checked in regularly. If he changed his brand of orange juice, I'd hear about it, and by now I figured what I hadn't heard was implied. Sometimes I said to people, Though I'm not and never have been Walter's wife, I often play the *role* of Walter's wife.

"We can't find Lorraine," he said. "She told us 9:00 and we were there at 8:45, but what else is new. So we've been walking around the neighborhood. We went into the market and the coffee shop and the dry cleaners and even the Zen meditation temple on the corner. We stopped in there."

"Looking for Lorraine," I said.

"I know, but it's been nearly an hour and a half. Anyway, we didn't find her in any of those places, but I swear we ran into every woman I ever slept with or even took out for a chaste cup of coffee during those two years of my divorce. I know I never told you about them, and I'm sorry about that, but the truth is there were a lot of women, and all of them are down here this morning walking in this neighborhood." His voice was high and short on breath. "It's uncanny," he said.

I was stung by the thought of all those women, though I had no reason to be. That I was not one of them was probably why Walter and I were still friends. Perhaps life required friends, like wives, to learn not to be hurt by what was necessary.

"You're quiet," Walter said. "Should I say I'm sorry again?"

"Don't embarrass me, Walter. You were in trouble and needed privacy. I get that."

"Oh, please. I was a coward, a needy coward, and too afraid to let you know me like that. What I don't understand is why I let a string of relative strangers know me like that."

"You should look over at Roy now, Walter. Can you still see him?"

"I'm telling you, he's right in front of me. I'm not taking my eyes off him. I'm the one who's stumbled into some condensed version of his past. You think that doesn't make a person hyper-vigilant? Roy," I heard him call. Then he said, "There. He's waving at me. What a sweetheart."

"Walter, put him in the car and come over here."

"I'm going to wait a little longer for Lorraine," he said. "And then I will. I just wanted to call, and frankly, I'm afraid to walk into the bakery for the glazed doughnut Roy wants. I hate to guess who might be waiting in there for me. Lord, what sort of man am I to have wanted all those women, to have had all those women? I shouldn't be walking a boy around by the hand, I'll tell you that."

"You were just looking for comfort," I said. "Lorraine could create a powerful need for comfort."

Immediately I was sorry for having said that because Walter said distantly, "She could, couldn't she," and I heard him falling further back into that time.

Lorraine drank—at first no more than anyone else, then enough to be witty and gay and the best dancer at any party. Then it became her vocation; Walter's shortly became to clean up after her. Who knew why they stayed together? He'd asked me often enough, and always I thought of their wedding party, held on a bitter night in the stuffy front room of their overheated bungalow. After the toasts and the cake and the mingling Walter and Lorraine collapsed on the couch while guests pulled folding chairs into a tight circle around them. Smoothing the folds of her dress, patting her pearls, Lorraine looked flushed and dewy in the heat. When Walter got up to fiddle again with the radiator she leaned her head back on the couch and said, "Oh, I wish someone would sing to me. I wish someone would sing *On the Street Where You Live*. Doesn't anyone know that song?"

The guests quieted. We weren't singers. No one sang at our parties. Then from the dining room, in full voice, Walter began. Lorraine raised her head, and he appeared in the archway, where he stood in his dark wedding suit and tie and sang, suddenly gifted with pitch and memory for even the obscure verses, over our heads to her. Lots of people, I told Walter whenever he asked, went blind that night.

Roy, miraculously born perfect, was Walter's salvation, and because Walter knew he couldn't count on more than one miracle in a lifetime, he applied for enough credit cards to finance a lawyer who could get him and Roy out of there. It took two years, during which Lorraine got worse and worse, until her bad behavior closely approximated madness. Once she turned on the gas and tried to explode the house with all of them in it. That's when a judge let Walter take Roy away, and that's when Lorraine stopped the drinking, the bad behavior, everything. Once Walter and Roy were gone, she said, she understood that was what she'd wanted all along. Even now she only asked to see the boy once or twice a year. The visits always made Walter a little crazy with guilt and worry, and sent him headlong into his past, like today.

"You know what I just realized," Walter said. "I'm calling from the exact phone I used whenever I sneaked out to call my lawyer after she threatened to murder me in my sleep."

"Walter, get out of there." I felt the grip of my own secrets, called out from wherever my body kept them by the close company of Walter's and Bette's and Belinda's, and what they accomplished inside me I suddenly didn't know—except to squeeze out space for decent feeling and vital organs. "Hang up and come on over."

"I don't know," he said.

I understood that he couldn't move. Even the memory of the madness with Lorraine required that he find immediate comfort, so I said, as firmly as I knew how, "Who better than you, Walter, to see Roy through the trouble he has ahead? Who knows more than you about navigating the life waiting for that boy."

Behind him, I heard the street, the buses and the passersby and the cars. On the other side of that, I thought, was Roy, waiting on a bench. Walter spoke softly.

"Say that again," he said. "Say it slow this time so I'll remember."

The Iowa Short Fiction Award and John Simmons Short Fiction Award Winners

2004
What You've Been Missing,
Janet Desaulniers
Here Beneath Low-Flying Planes, Merrill Feitell

2003
Bring Me Your Saddest Arizona,
Ryan Harty
American Wives, Beth Helms

2002
Her Kind of Want,
Jennifer S. Davis
The Kind of Things Saints Do,
Laura Valeri

2001
Ticket to Minto: Stories of India and America,
Sohrab Homi Fracis
Fire Road, Donald Anderson

2000
Articles of Faith, Elizabeth Oness
Troublemakers, John McNally

1999
House Fires, Nancy Reisman
Out of the Girls' Room and into the Night,
Thisbe Nissen

1998
Friendly Fire,
Kathryn Chetkovich
The River of Lost Voices: Stories from Guatemala,
Mark Brazaitis

1997
Thank You for Being Concerned and Sensitive,
Jim Henry
Within the Lighted City,
Lisa Lenzo

1996
Hints of His Mortality,
David Borofka
Western Electric, Don Zancanella

1995
Listening to Mozart,
Charles Wyatt
May You Live in Interesting Times,
Tereze Glück

1994
The Good Doctor,
Susan Onthank Mates
Igloo among Palms,
Rod Val Moore

1993
Happiness, Ann Harleman
Macauley's Thumb,
Lex Williford
Where Love Leaves Us,
Renée Manfredi

1992
My Body to You,
Elizabeth Searle
Imaginary Men, Enid Shomer